Praise for Christopher Brookhouse

"Brookhouse is fascinated by the textures of everyday life in the past, as Lenny faces each day in a small town in the era of Camaros and the triumph of Billie Jean King. ... [*How It Was*] glances against [the complexities of inter-racial attraction] ... plus true-to-life complications involving tutoring and academic honesty without losing its sure footing..."

— PW Booklife —

"Th[is] character-driven narrative focuses not so much on generating excitement as on painting compelling portraits. [In *A Mind of Winter,*] Brookhouse writes with a gentle charm, expressed through edgy, efficient dialogue and tightly constructed prose that uses single moments to create vivid snapshots that propel the story forward at a languid but deliberate pace..."

— Kirkus Reviews —

[*Messing with Men*] ... follows aging residents in a resort town as they fall in and out of love and lust with each other, dabble in local causes, and try to make sense of their lives...These wryly reflective Floridian retirees, with their longings and regrets, will remain with readers.

—PW Booklife—

"Brookhouse's writing is so good and so elegant ... [*Percy's Field*] is not a fast-paced thriller that emphasizes action. Rather, this novel moves slowly in the Carolina humidity, and the emphasis is placed on the immaculate prose and the deep characterization given to Harr County and North Carolina's tobacco country. ... The book excels at presenting a dark and enjoyable murder story that resonates with the truth that the past is never really over."

— from a *Foreword* Clarion Review —

"*FINN* is the real thing—a southern Gothic tale in which the narrator must solve the mystery of his own nature in order to escape the web of violence in which he is caught. Start it when you have time to finish because you won't want to put it down."

— Terry Roberts, author of
A Short Time to Stay Here and winner of the
Willie Morris Award for Southern Fiction

"[*FINN* is a] novel to be savored more than once. Written with the same languorous, rumbling passion of Paul Newman and Joanne Woodward's film *The Long Hot Summer*."

— Kirkus Reviews —

"[*Silence* is a] memorable story by a talented writer who understands women better than most women understand themselves."

— Doris Betts —

"[*Silence*] is a quiet novel of personal and seasonal challenges set in a small town in New Hampshire. Brookhouse writes confidently and unobtrusively about authentic issues."

— Kirkus Reviews —

"Christopher Brookhouse has produced another literary wonder in *Old-Timer*. It is both easy to read and playfully complex."

— Rob Neufeld —
Asheville Citizen-Times

"[*Old-Timer* is one] of the best novel releases by one of the best authors you haven't heard about."

— Tom Mayer —
New Bern Sun Journal

Finding Plymm

CHRISTOPHER BROOKHOUSE

SHB Safe Harbor Books
Marshall, N.C.
a publisher of photography and fiction

Safe Harbor Books
1293 Boulder Rd.
Marshall, NC 28753
www.safeharborbooks.com

First Edition

ISBN: 978-1-7344995-4-4 (trade paperback)

ISBN: 978-1-7344995-5-1 (eBook)

Library of Congress Cataloging-in-Publication Data

Names: Brookhouse, Christopher, 1938- author.
Title: Finding Plymm / Christopher Brookhouse.
Description: First Edition. | Marshall, N.C. : Safe Harbor Books, 2024. |
Summary: "Theo Vos comes to Mott County from Ohio in search of answers about an ancestor whose casket had been shipped home during the Civil War but when it arrived, the body inside wasn't his. While there, Vos is hired to tutor an agoraphobic teenager, the only child of Milo and Calla Drew. Milo, a once renowned author, has holed himself up in the family castle too, working on a book based on an old journal of the county's sheriff during the War Between the States. "Finding Plymm" weaves back and forth between Theo's growing place in the community and Milo's typewritten imagination. Only the reader knows for sure, but the answer to Theo's mystery may just be under his nose"-- Provided by publisher.
Identifiers: LCCN 2024007707 (print) | LCCN 2024007708 (ebook) | ISBN 9781734499544 (trade paperback) | ISBN 9781734499551 (eBook)
Subjects: LCGFT: Novels.
Classification: LCC PS3552.R658 F54 2024 (print) | LCC PS3552.R658 (ebook) | DDC 813/.54--dc23/eng/20240216
LC record available at https://lccn.loc.gov/2024007707
LC ebook record available at https://lccn.loc.gov/2024007708

Cover art adapted from "River Reflections 2"
by David Skinner, www.dskinner.net

Printed in the USA.

Dedication

For Vally, whose sharp eye and computer savvy
have made publishing possible.
Whose dedication and friendship
have made it a pleasure.

I
Mott County, North Carolina
1990

His name was Vos. Hers Drew. The great fireplace had warmed generations of Drews as they stood at the tall windows and watched deer browse the dark slope of the orchard and snow blur the summits of the distant mountains. This October afternoon no fire burned. Autumn light lost its way in the clutter of tables and chairs, highboys, and couches. A chill filled the room. People said the house had its own weather.

Calla Drew wore the wool sweater her sister had sent from Dublin and the suede trousers mailed from a boutique in Milan. Theo Vos's plaid shirt was frayed at the elbows, his jeans at the knees. He dressed, she thought, no better than the young men who drifted into the county, worked menial jobs when they felt like it, claiming to be free from the toxins of capitalism. Better looking, though. Delicate features. Lovely blue eyes. Could use a decent pair of shoes. His were coming apart.

"I suppose you know Jefferson from the tavern," she said. Jefferson—her husband's half-brother, one of their father's mistakes.

"We meet there."

"Ordinarily I wouldn't give much thought to anyone he recommended, but Miss Tripp at the college said you were eminently qualified. Since you had declined its offer of employment, she was curious why you would consider tutoring my daughter. I'm not going to pay you a professor's salary." Founded by Baptists, the tiny college had given up its Christian mission in favor of any curriculum a student decided to pursue and could pay for. By the tenth grade, most of the local children had dropped out of school, many for a paycheck, a few for the brief freedom of recreational medications. "Even the pittance a third-rate college like ours pays," Calla said.

"I rent a cabin near the bypass. Cold nights snakes crawl inside. One was in my bed."

A cot, Calla imagined. Or a sleeping bag, no sheets. Miss Tripp probably had decent sheets. They probably required frequent washing if the rumors about her were true. Calla heard Theo had stayed with her, one of many. Miss Tripp—Professor Tripp—wasn't much for confidentiality.

"There are rooms in town. Furnished. No reptiles."

"I'm not enthusiastic about my own cooking."

So that was it. "The position here provides room and board." Calla was five feet six. He an inch taller. She guessed she outweighed him by twenty pounds. "You're on the slender side. Mrs. Garth, our housekeeper and cook, serves generous helpings."

He nodded as if his thoughts were somewhere else.

"What about your private life? I assume you have one. Professor Tripp implied you did." If half of what Calla had heard were true, at a decent college Tripp would be out on her ear—or the body part she flaunted under the especially skimpy skirts she wore. "We would need to have an understanding about your comings and goings. No disappearing every night and returning at dawn like a satiated vampire."

"Once a week?"

"Are you trying to be funny?"

"Yes."

How rude. "What kind of name is Vos?"

"Dutch."

"You know Dutch?"

"I'm better at French or Spanish. Some Latin."

"You've travelled?"

"Here and there."

"Why here?"

"Research."

She heard the ticking of the tall clock in the hall. Theo had arrived half an hour ago. It seemed longer. "Mr. Vos, are you guarding a secret?"

"Ma'am?"

"Researching what?"

"An ancestor."

"And Jefferson is assisting your research?"

"He knows local history, old property lines, vanished homeplaces, graves hidden in the grass. The rumors and stories that go with them. Those sorts of things."

"I don't want to speak ill of my brother-in-law, but Jefferson has never had a proper job. He considers himself the guardian of local culture. He has enough family money to operate a gallery displaying the efforts of our local painters and potters and such. Every so often a lost tourist buys something. He even sold one of his own photographs—a sad-eyed girl in a ragged dress holding her pet goose. Black and white. Gloomy indeed."

"I saw one he took of Martha."

The clock struck the quarter hour. The light was going out of the sky. "Let's get to the point. Martha is sixteen, almost seventeen. She won't leave the house. As you're aware, it's a very big house, plenty of space for her to make her own world. Her therapists cautioned me not to force the outdoors upon her or her upon it."

"Are you employing me?"

"Mr. Vos, what choice do I have? It's been months since I've spoken with a suitable candidate. You probably know that Milo, Martha's father, is a writer. When he takes an interest in her, he fills her mind with all sorts of myths and stories. That's got to change."

"What were the previous tutors like?"

"Dry sticks, who didn't live in. Retired clergy or professors needing an extra buck to supplement their pensions and had little interest in Martha, whom they considered frivolous and spoiled. Except for the last one. Jefferson convinced me to hire a student from the college. He took a shine to her. I dismissed him. Be warned, Mister...what should I call you?"

"Theodore, but I prefer Theo. And you?"

"Calla, but I prefer Mrs. Drew. Let's agree to meet tomorrow and work out schedules, compensation, living arrangements, et cetera. The Laurel. Noon?"

Theo followed her to the front door. She said, "Noon, I mean it. Don't be late."

"I'll be early." He smiled as if what he was thinking amused him.

"Will you have much...what's the Latin word for luggage?"

"*Impedimenta*. Not much," he said.

Jefferson Drew pushed the basket of breadsticks aside and handed the book across the table. *Wells Guide to the Western Counties*, 1913 edition, open to a photograph captioned Dolley's Tavern, Elland, Mott County, where Jefferson and Theo sat waiting for Connie to bring them their drinks. Wells had noted the county's reputation for producing excellent whiskey while eschewing the collection of federal taxes. Before voters had recently approved selling alcohol by the drink, the tavern had sold only beer and inferior wine. Now, however, all sorts of pricey spirits in lovely bottles were available. Connie and Belva, the other server, who formerly wore jeans and shapeless T-shirts advertising rock concerts or NASCAR events, now dressed in black tapered trousers and dark blue shirts with the tavern's name stitched in pink letters above the pocket. Ralph, the owner, thought the combination of colors subtle and attractive. Like a bruise, Connie said.

"Page one-thirteen." Theo found the page and a sketch of the Drew house—called the Castle: three stories tall, twenty-seven rooms, forbidding stone walls, a sloped roof of clay tiles. "Takes the cake for ugly and gloomy," Jefferson said. "If Calla gives you a choice of rooms, avoid anything on the north side. It's always cold, although the ones on the third floor have good views of the river."

"Gentlemen…" Connie lowered her tray. "Vodka clear and pure as a potent mind," she said and set Theo's glass on the table. "Whiskey fragrant and dark with wisdom from fine old barrels," she said and handed Jefferson his glass.

Jefferson smiled up at her while caressing her hip. "Fancy language. What have you been reading?"

"One of your brother's books."

"Which one?"

"*Thatch*. At the end of our seminar, Milo gave each of us a copy, signed plus a little verse. Mine was 'As you go hence, Beware the present tense. Another recommendation, Adjectives in moderation.' All three of us. Not the college's most popular course."

"Wasn't him who convinced you to drop out, was it?"

"Wasn't *he*. No, the dean of the college did. The A your brother gave me didn't convince her to overlook the several D's and F's I had racked up in two point five years of higher education."

"Milo said you were a good writer." He had also commented on her generous mouth, shapely thighs, and firm breasts, which Jefferson could praise as well from personal experience.

"I earned the A for my work, not for sleeping with him."

"Did you?"

"I made myself available, but he said, 'I go no more a roving'." Connie reached behind her, lifted Jefferson's hand, and directed it toward his whiskey. "Don't let it go to your head." Halfway back to the bar, she turned and aired him a kiss.

"What was all that about?" Theo asked.

"Have you met Milo?"

"I believe I glimpsed him through a window. A hunched figure at a desk staring at a typewriter."

"The satyr in his lair. Originally a side parlor used only when a family member died and guests were invited to imbibe strong drink while they viewed the body reposing in its casket."

"Satyrs have a bit of age. Does Milo qualify?"

"He's fifty-three. I'm thirty-nine, though I like to think I play younger. Connie has other ideas. It's not sex with her that has my attention as much as the games we play getting there. The preamble lasts for weeks. The sex itself is kind of a one-act thing."

"How old is Mrs. Drew?"

"Calla is forty-three, but she plays older." Jefferson took a long drink and looked off. "If she plays at all. She's a bit of a snob. College up north took the South out of her."

People Jefferson had never seen crowded the room. He finished his whiskey and raised his empty glass. This time Ralph came over—a large man in his sixties wearing boots, jeans, apron, plaid shirt, sleeves rolled up. Tattoo of a shield and spear.

"Leaf peepers," Ralph said, "all excited to visit a county known for its mountain music, outlaw ways, quaint speech, and vicious home brew." He pointed to the book on the table. "That man is responsible for some of the nonsense."

Jefferson watched a woman in a sequined denim jacket and short skirt studying the selections on the restored Wurlitzer. "Not sure whose responsibility she is, but I'd like to find out."

"Younger than the others or rich enough to afford better skin conditioners," Ralph said. He stared at Theo. "You're not from here… what do you think? Is Mott County still full of enough uncivilized cranks to satisfy tourists' expectations?"

"You need fewer bikers and kayakers decked out in designer wear and more toothless locals like the one outside the post office who spits tobacco and talks to himself."

"Watch your words. That's Homer. He's a cousin of mine." Ralph picked up the empty glasses. "But you're right. The county is changing. Besides the usual riffraff, folks with education and money are moving in. Cheap, lovely land won't be around much longer."

Belva brought refills and menus. "You might need to feed yourself. Maintain your stamina. I've been saving up mine." She winked and walked back to the bar.

"You could do worse. And I'm not talking victuals," Jefferson said.

"I haven't been *doing* like you mean it at all."

"No more Tripping?"

"Some professor caught her eye. But she recommended me for the tutorial job."

"Our nights here may be limited. Calla disapproves of Dolley's, a stain on the reputation of a first lady who was the model of grace, civility, and propriety. None of which can be found here—thank God. Calla may declare Dolley's off-limits if you want to keep your job. Wells points out that the man who designed the Drew residence also did prisons."

"Your point?"

"Don't let yourself be a prisoner. Negotiate."

"I haven't met Martha yet, only seen the photograph you showed me. Tripp says she has a keen mind and an active imagination. Any advice?"

"Be careful," Jefferson said. "There's a lot going on in that keen mind of hers."

Theo watched him cross the room and introduce himself to the woman who stood in the floating glow of the Wurlitzer's lights while Patti Page lamented losing her darling the night they were playing the Tennessee waltz. Ralph banned songs that weren't country or were written after 1970.

Belva leaned over Theo's shoulder. "What's it going to be?"

"I can't decide between a burger or pizza."

"That's not what I meant," she said.

"I was counting on you to say that," he said.

"WHAT'S HE LIKE? MARTHA ASKED.

Eunice Garth had taken away the breakfast dishes, leaving Calla and Martha alone. Out the window Calla saw Milo and Duncan, the spaniel, limping in front of him on their way to the orchard. The apple trees still produced, but the plums were scaly skeletons, and the peaches, always a challenge, had long ago given up and become habitat for squirrels and birds. He stopped to light one of the small cigars he smoked. "Disgusting," Calla said about the cigar, louder than she meant to speak.

"He's disgusting?"

"I'm sure not. He appears…" Likable? she thought. Handsome? He was that. Intelligent? "He could use a good meal."

"Will he be living with us?"

"Our arrangements are pending."

"Will Miss Nadir like him?" Martha mimed brushing back her hair and pretended to hold a cigarette as if posing for a celebrity photograph.

Of all her daughter's imaginary friends, Miss Nadir was Calla's least favorite. "I'm sure she will approve."

"She expects better than the one the student stud service sent over."

Where did Martha get this stuff—student stud service? One of Milo's books?

"The man is Mr. Vos. Theodore Vos. You're welcome to accompany me to the Laurel and meet him yourself."

"Impossible. My schedule is full."

"Doing what?"

Martha turned to her right and looked up. "Miss Grimm, what am I doing?"

Grimm—she was new.

"I remember now." Martha turned back at Calla. "With Grimm's help I'm creating a guest list for my birthday party and having a pedicure. The studly tutor wanted to suck my toes."

Had he really or had Martha dreamed it? "Could we forget him?"

"For the moment."

"Would you like a party?"

"I prefer presents, no cake. No food at all. Only drinks. Bloody Marys."

"Miss Nadir told me you wanted a car for your birthday."

"She erred. Why would I want a vehicle? I would need to go outside to use it. I don't drive."

"You could learn."

"Mr. Jonah advises against it."

"You haven't mentioned him for a while."

"He's been away. A boat trip. It didn't go well."

"But he's back. Safe and sound?"

"Avoid whales, he says."

"I won't invite any."

Martha stood. Blonde and shapely. Like a young Grace Kelly. A knockout, the studly tutor had called her. "Come, Miss Grimm," Martha said and held out her hand.

Once the stately home of the Stock family, the Laurel—a subdued example of Second Empire architecture—now tilting precariously on a rocky hillside above the town, was the only accommodation for travelers other than the Cozy Corner motel on the bypass. Wilfred Stock kept four rooms to rent—three on the second floor, one with its own bath. The two others shared a bathroom.

A courtly octogenarian, barely five feet tall with white hair to his shoulders, Wilfred called the tower room on the third floor a suite, by which he meant it was a sweet place for a man to enjoy female companionship as long as one avoided the draft around the dormer and didn't bump one's head against the slant of mansard roof or feel inconvenienced by navigating the creaking stairs to descend to the bathroom on the floor below. Wilfred employed a Black cook who turned out remarkably good meals. Her biscuits and omelets were famous. On court days the restaurant was packed.

As Wilfred himself opened the ornate double door to welcome Calla, Belva was just leaving. She bent down and kissed his cheek. "Delightful, as always," she said. She paused to look back and wave at Theo, who had stopped in the hall to admire a framed sketch of the town on Election Day 1872 as observed from the porch of the Laurel, a scene of general rowdiness. Pennants flew from tents where men bought the alcohol the county was renowned for or the services of women imported from Holcombe, the next county over.

Calla and Belva nodded to each other. Wilfred escorted Calla to a table in the dining room, Theo trailing behind. He glimpsed himself in one of the mirrors, dark where the silver had flaked off. He considered himself presentable, bathed and shaved, and wearing new boots and jeans. Belva had lent him her special narcissus soap. After Mason, their waiter, had brought water and menus, Calla sniffed, stared at Theo, and remarked he smelled flowery. Otherwise, she assumed, his skin might present the fragrance of conjugal activity. Something more in her past than her present.

They ordered. Mason came and went. Calla spoke of the long-standing friendship between the Stocks and the Drews. Once the two most influential families in the county, now Wilfred depended on the whims of strangers or the assignations of locals for income. Despite the expenses of maintaining an historic property, the Drews were financially well off. Calla aimed to keep it that way. She had a head for investments. Milo was content to hide himself in his parlor and peck out a few words a day on a novel that few would buy (the recent ones hadn't sold well), and Martha, who had the body of a young Grace Kelly, had the mind of a...well, she was witty and troubled—afraid of bushes and trees and space. Then there was Jefferson. He didn't count.

Calla warned Theo that sometimes her husband emerged from his den and roamed the house, conversing with paintings or furniture, items connected to the past. She was grateful he no longer gave a seminar at the college since that meant he no longer strayed, but a husband who only showed up for meals was a bit of a drag even if the soup was served in two-hundred-year-old Sèvres.

They finished the meal with coffee. Calla named a salary. Theo agreed to it. He could have his choice of rooms. Wednesdays and Sundays were free days. Others he should be a tutor and a companion to Martha. Nights he could stay in or go out. He was not to have company at the house. He would take his meals in the kitchen. Alcohol in moderation. No drugs, even if marijuana was a cash crop in Mott County.

One last concern. "If Martha visits your room, the door must remain open." He was not to go to hers. She had seemed a bit too interested in the attentions of the man the college stud service had supplied.

1865

Two weeks since news of the surrender had spread through the valley. We heard rumors that Mr. Lincoln was dead. The company colonel thanked us for our service and loyalty to our country and told us to make our way home. We were in east Tennessee. Ohio and Indiana, where Albert was from, were a far walk. Albert thought it best to avoid roads, if there were any. Follow the paths of carts and horses. We would find enough of those. We threw away anything conspicuous or useless like our forage caps or fry pans. We weren't going to do much cooking.

About the first day of May, we figured. It started cold and cloudy. Spits of rain. Faired off and warmed. Saw no one. Night, we crossed a field and made out a barn and a cabin. We heard music. A party of some kind.

We reckoned we had strayed into North Carolina. According to the penciled map on a square of smudged paper we had, Mott County, a place of scattered farms and villages, Elland being the county seat, most residents supporting the rebel cause, and us in our uniforms. Our shirts and drawers were the only garments we provided for ourselves, and those were worn through. If we had seen clothing that fit us, we weren't against a bit of thieving, but the chance of being shot made us honest men.

Fiddle music, Albert said. We supposed it's what people here were accustomed to. Sounded nice. We studied how the lanterns on the cabin's porch fingered light across ground between us and the barn.

We hunkered and watched couples laughing and dancing. A celebration, we thought. A bearded man holding a jug swayed down the steps. By a tree close to us, he set the jug on the ground and urinated. A woman stood on the steps but didn't follow him into the dark. She called out his name. He called back that he was waiting for her. She told him to wait some more. Her voice was light and lovely, inviting. I could imagine sweet pastimes she'd be sharing. The smell of a woman, long time since I'd breathed that. Best we keep moving, Albert said.

In the distance we heard flowing water, probably not the big river called French Broad on our map. Likely a creek. Lucky with the rain if it was pure enough to fill our canteens. The wind had turned south. Rain about to start up again. We had enough hardtack and dried fruit to feed us a couple more days. We had learned to make cooch from the rebels. Albert didn't think he'd ever miss it, but he did now.

Just before the rain began, we scuttled through a thicket of rhododendron and found shelter under an overhang of pitted rock. Think there is snakes? Albert asked. I told him to think about something else, like the woman on the steps. She was still on my mind. I lay on my back, my finger stroking the hollow of hair under my arm.

All night a hard rain. Albert woke before I did. He was reading in the Bible I had lent him. He had given his to a wounded private from our company, a man named Smith, who had lost his own. Albert was Catholic, though he never told anyone but me and made me swear never to tell it to anyone else. I prayed for Smith, he said, and crossed himself. Better start, I said. We plodded through bramble and mud, making our way along the tree line above a river so wide it must be the French Broad. The oaks weren't leafed yet, but the willows near the water were green.

The sun high, we sprawled in tall grass. Words of Bryant I had memorized came back to me. "The sweet breeze That makes the green leaves dance Shall waft a balm to thy sick heart." It was so. We unbuttoned our jackets and watched the clouds change shapes as if we were free of "sorrows, crimes, and cares." Despite the runoff, the river ran clean. Albert told me he did not care how cold the water might be, he wanted to wash all over. Maybe catch a fish with his bare hands. Bragged he could do that.

I raised up and watched him strip and wade into the water. Another man stepped into the light, like he'd been close to us all the time. He wore only his drawers and carried his pants in his right hand by his side. A scabbard dangled from the belt. He poked at Albert's uniform with his foot.

Albert had said we had a long way to go. Why carry a rifle? But I didn't mind what the Enfield weighed, so I had paid to keep it. I tore open the cartridge pack, rammed down the powder and mini ball, and set the cap in place. I sighted the rifle at the man on the shore watching Albert step slowly out of the water. The man held his pants behind him now. He reached his left hand back and eased a bayonet from the scabbard. The pants fell out of his right, which he offered to Albert, as if to greet a stranger. Then the man lunged and stood looking down at Albert bleeding at his feet. Birds flew up and scattered. The echo of the Enfield died away.

I closed Albert's eyes and said a prayer. The rifle across my knees, I rested awhile, thinking, making up my mind. I laid the rifle aside and set about my task. I dressed the man in my trousers and buckled the belt and dragged his body into the grass. Wasn't time to search for his shirt or his brogans. Then I pulled Albert's pants up his legs, tugged his body into the river, and let it float away. Finally, I fit myself into the dead man's pants. I emptied my haversack of most everything I could carry and left it and my jacket and bedroll near the body. I threw Albert's shirt, brogans, jacket, and pack into the river along with the dead man's bayonet and scabbard. Up the rocky hill I found a hollow place between slabs of rock to hide the Enfield, my cartridge pouch, and cap box. Too late I remembered my Bible.

II

Martha leaned in the doorway. "Did Caesar go to England?"

Theo was making his bed. "Good morning to you, and yes, he did."

"Why?"

"It was Roman territory. I think he wanted to warn people who didn't like that to back off and stop causing trouble."

"A long way from home, wasn't he?"

"A bit."

"Is this your home now?"

"As long as your mother employs me."

"Calla, you mean? She's not my mother. Earth is, but she doesn't like me much. When Calla carried me home from the hospital, there was a quake. Not a catastrophic one like a hundred years ago that wiped out forests and moved rivers, but the road split open. Earth's warning. I stay inside to keep out of her way. Who is *your* mother?"

"Katherine. Katherine Vos."

"No, your deep mother. Not fire, I think. Probably water. Do you like water?"

"To drink."

"I presume you bathe."

"I do."

Martha edged into the room. She wore a fringed shirt, leggings, and moccasins. She was tall and blonde and every bit as lovely as

Theo thought she would be from Jefferson's photo of her. "Did you choose this room because you can see the river?"

"That was one reason."

"Do you know why it's called the French Broad?"

"You tell me."

"Big rivers were called broads. This one flows into Tennessee, which used to be French territory. At least that's what Pete said."

"Pete was your tutor?"

"Pistil Pete. I'm sure Calla mentioned him. He was from the college. He stuck his hand down my shirt. He said I weirded him."

"What's that mean?"

"Excited him…you know. I bet Calla warned you."

"What did you learn from him?"

"I liked…Are you referring to the shirt thing or something else?"

"Do you prefer to discuss specific subjects at specific times?"

"I don't like schedules or assignments. Some of this, some of that. You talk, I listen. Listen and learn. I *abhor*—such a lovely word, almost naughty—I abhor mathematics."

"You can add, subtract, and multiply, though?"

"Of course. Also, basic algebra and geometry—stuff like that. Do you know how long it takes light to travel from the sun to the earth?"

"Not exactly."

"Eight minutes and twenty seconds."

"I'll keep that in mind. What do you do for books?"

"Daddy's library. He helps me pick and choose. Some of his books I'm not supposed to know about, but I do."

"How?"

"I prefer not to say."

"Any textbooks?"

"Some somewhere. The county sent Calla a home-school kit."

"Biology?"

"The monk—"

"Mendel?"

"Yes, he and his peas were interesting. Pistil Pete liked to discuss reproduction. P I S T I L, not P I S T O L."

"Let's call him Pete."

"May I call you Theo and skip the Vos part? What's it mean?"

"Guess."

"Voice?"

"Animal."

"Fox?"

"Right. Call me Theo."

"Call me Ishmael. *Moby Dick* is the longest book I've read. I found it a bit tiresome. I like Hawthorne better, all those gloomy shades and forests. Did you know he added the *h* to the family name?

"I do now. Thanks."

"Pete was science. No poetry in him. Milo—Daddy—has lots of it. You'll hear him roaming the house at night, reciting bits of this and that—when he's not conversing with inanimate objects. He drinks. Calla said you do too, with Uncle Jefferson."

"We're friends."

"Has Miss Nadir been to meet you?"

"Who is she?"

"My friend. She finds the help tedious. Try to please her."

"How would I do that?"

"She likes people telling stories about themselves. Last night Jonah was describing what it was like inside a whale. Dark and slippery. Bit of an odor. He went on and on about despair and getting coughed up. Sticky, he said."

"How will I recognize Miss Nadir?"

"She prefers to attire herself in fur. She finds the heating system dismal."

Theo and Martha stood by the window now. In the distance Milo was smoking and walking Duncan, the hapless spaniel.

TIMOTHY HARMON, MD. PEOPLE trusted Dr. Tim. Three generations of his family had farmed in the county. His parents hoped he would become a large-animal veterinarian, but people interested him more than cows and mules, and the mind interested him more than the heart (in a physical sense). He always ended a routine examination with a chat about the patient's personal life.

The simplicity of Dr. Tim's personal life was reassuring to the community. No fancy office. He drove a Ford not a Cadillac or an import. He wore black shoes with cushioned soles, chinos, and an oxford shirt, no matter the season. No stethoscope around his neck, no emblem of authority that set him apart and made him special, at least in his own mind. Some considered him a bit dour, though. His office at the back of his house a block off Main Street lacked magazines, plants, or even a small collection of children's picture books to distract and entertain his youngest patients. In thirty years of practice, he had employed two nurses and one accountant. He had never married. The rumor that he and his housekeeper, Mary Turner, were intimate satisfied people's curiosity about his sexual inclinations, even adding a useful touch of mystery to his reputation. He was fifty-seven. Lots of good years left and money in the bank. Several widows eyed him as a man they might lure into marriage, the problem being that the usual enticements, such as wealth, travel, or social standing, did not tempt him, and none of the widows could compete with the skills Mary had learned and perfected in the years of her own practice.

The office was warm. Calla took off her silk jacket and laid it across her lap. "Your labs are excellent," Dr. Tim said. "How is your life in general?"

"Milo is the same, but at least he's working. Or I think he is. I hear his typewriter clacking away. If he learned to use a computer, I wouldn't hear anything. Not sure I'd like that. He might drop dead, and I wouldn't know about it."

"How is he with Martha?"

"I wanted a child. He did his part. Our agreement always was he or she would be my responsibility. But I do think he loves her."

"His part—has he given up on that?"

"Do we have sex? Not for a while."

Dr. Tim opened Calla's folder. "You're forty-three. You're not ready to call it quits, are you?"

"I'm used to it."

"Any changes with Martha?"

"I wish. I hope you don't stop making house calls. Her therapist did. Said it wasn't professional. Part of Martha's therapy was her showing up at his office."

"He has a point."

"Martha has a new tutor—Theo Vos. Know him?"

"I gave him a tetanus booster."

"He hangs out with my brother-in-law at Dolley's. I'm not keen on the company they keep. I assume there's not a local outbreak of what we used to call a social disease."

"None I'm aware of." Dr. Tim tapped Calla's folder on his knee. "Where did you and Milo meet?"

"At a writers' conference. Back then he was a major attraction. A best-seller and a movie. He was a different man then—energetic, outgoing, sexy, sober."

"You wanted to be a writer?"

"I was interested in the business of writing. I should have tried New York, become an agent or an editor or whatever."

"You wouldn't have liked New York."

"My sister lives there. Her husband does something international. They travel a lot. She sends me gifts from all over." Calla held up her jacket.

"Would you like to travel?"

"Who would care for Milo and Martha?"

"Perhaps they could care for each other."

"What an odd sense of humor you have."

"Most people don't think I have any."

Calla left Dr. Tim's office and sat in her car, a Buick. Milo's father had bought Buicks, so Milo did too, although the only driving he did anymore was to Holcombe County for whiskey. Why Mott County residents had voted to allow bars to sell liquor by the drink but vetoed having a state store that sold spirits by the bottle was not only a contradiction but an inconvenience. According to Milo, the vote against state stores was meant to protect local distillers and honor the county's tradition of bootlegging that was now more a fact of history than a feature of everyday life.

Calla sat in the car and thought about the question Dr. Tim never asked, though she was sure it was the one foremost in his mind: How can you stay married to Milo and live cooped up in the Castle? Well, I love him, she would answer. Not entirely a lie. She had loved him from the start, the author standing before an audience of would-be writers enraptured by his soft, Southern voice reading from his novel whose success was what they dreamed would befall their own work.

She was not bashful, not brought up to be, only schooled to cloak her desires with charm and innocence. In the wealthy Tidewater society into which she was born, a young woman, if offered a drink from the flask her beau brought forth from his white dinner jacket as the couple walked under the oaks edging the fairway of the county club course, she would coyly say, "Oh, I shouldn't" or "Do you have in mind taking advantage of me, sir?" when she wanted the drink very much and intended to take advantage of him.

On her seventeenth birthday Calla decided it was time to lose her virginity, but not to someone her age, a young man who lacked experience and would embellish the event and boast about it to his friends. One didn't want one's name to be bandied about, or worse, to appear on a bathroom wall. With caution and design disguised as naivete, Calla gave herself to a friend of her father's, a man whose unhappy spouse would have used his infidelity for significant financial gain had she discovered it. He, convinced he had been the seducer and not the seduced, provided a useful sexual prologue to which Calla would often refer to guide her with other lovers. The man assuaged his guilt by giving Calla a lovely emerald bracelet, which she hid until she left for college and later sold when her family's fortune took a turn for the worse. All their fields and forests gone to developers. The stables torn down. The art and antiques auctioned. The house turned into a hospice. At least the legacies Calla and her sister received from grandparents survived, and, out of necessity, both sisters learned to manage money well.

Security, then, Calla would have answered had Dr. Tim asked why she stuck with Milo. Money was more important than sex. Nevertheless, she missed it. Dr. Tim was right. She was too young to give it up. Milo hadn't, or only with her, something she did not understand except that sex for him had to satisfy his imagination. His partners had to fit into a narrative of some kind. Once she had done that. Now, though, she was too real, was merely mundane reality. He had sold his virginity to a broad-shouldered country woman, who accepted five silver dollars for her services. She still serviced Milo's favorite fantasy. His flings with students were peripheral and momentary. They didn't fit the fantasy. Mrs. Garth did, but Calla pretended she didn't know about that relationship. Pretending not to know was a far greater favor and kindness than knowing and accepting it.

MILO POURED HIMSELF A whiskey, then leaned over his typewriter and found where he had left off.

What should I call you? the woman asked. Plymm, I said. I told her I had come a distance. You be hungry then, she said. I glanced about and saw no one, only the cow in the pasture, a few chickens, and the cabin, the roof needing repair. I heard hogs, though. Smelled them too. Their pen was on the other side of the barn.

The woman wore a calico dress. She stood tall and barefoot. No bonnet. Face brown. Eyes gray. She must cut her hair herself, I thought, uneven and shaggy as it was. Where you from, Plymm? East, I answered. Town called Bath. I'd seen the name on a map, and it stuck in my mind. She had heard of it. Been a while since I had one, she said. I was serving in Tennessee, I said. From your butternut britches I reckon which side you took. War's done now, I said. She nodded and asked if I would welcome some eggs and hominy. I thanked her for her kindness.

Her husband would be along before dark. He'd gone to town to settle something. He'd been wounded and lost an arm at the elbow. Could still manage a horse, if they had one. Ramsey, the mule, was left.

Her name was Nandina. Tates her husband's. She pointed to the roof. He had trouble keeping up with all that needed doing.

The cabin was one wide room: a chest, a stand of drawers, a bed, a table and shelves on the opposite side. Chairs, a loom, and a cradle faced the stone hearth. No stove like the iron one my family bought before the war began. Took three men to carry into the house. Nandina stirred the embers and laid on some slashings of wood.

What can I do? I asked. She frowned and considered the question as if it were complicated in some way, or the answer might be. Finally, she told me where the spring was. I would find a bucket on the porch.

The sun disappeared behind the mountain. Sometimes Tates gets to talking, she said. We'd best have our meal now. She poured something sweet over the collards she served along with the hominy and eggs. She didn't care for bitter.

What kind of work you do, she asked, when you're not soldiering? Taught children, I said, wondering if I would ever see the schoolhouse that was about the same size as the cabin again. You been to school then yourself, she said. I nodded. She smiled. Tell me. Don't be modest. A bit of college, I said.

She told me Tates could read and write and do sums. He used to recite songs, stories about lovers, misunderstandings, and such—folks getting drowned or poisoned. She pointed to the crib. Hester would have been her name, she said. Hester came out of me wrong. Tates has been different ever since.

Full dark. You don't need to be getting on tonight, do you? She showed me the barn. I climbed to the top of the hay and slept. The man and the mule woke me. Singing or mumbling, I wasn't sure, the man slid off the mule and staggered out of the stall. I heard him call Nandina's name into the night and a door slam shut.

Mrs. Garth would serve Theo's meal but not sit with him and eat hers. She would lean against the counter and observe as if he were foreign and different and might not hold a knife and fork like she did.

She was willing to talk, though. Tonight was Tuesday, which meant the missus would eat quickly and leave the house to meet with the Elland library committee, three other women who really got together to play bridge and discuss matters their husbands would not. Recently the main topics were what to do about the unsavory characters hanging around Dolley's and if Jefferson's gallery had gone too far by displaying a photograph of a famished child peering out of the window of a trailer parked in a cove above the river. Of course, one encountered poverty and hunger in the county, but why make art out of it—if one could call the image art.

"Martha's a handful and too smart for her own good," Mrs. Garth said. "Suffers from something unpronounceable, according to her therapist, the one who quit. Bright as she is, she's invented all manner of excuses and reasons to stay inside."

"Agoraphobia."

"I don't care what it's called. Someone should just yank her outside and tell her to live with it. What's your thought?"

"She wouldn't like that very much."

"The rest of us would. My sister, Mary, was afraid of water, wouldn't go near it. One day we had a family picnic, a place where the river runs slow and deep. Daddy picked Mary up and chucked her into the water. She learned to swim right quick, or at least to paddle and keep her head above water. For a while she and Daddy didn't speak, but that passed."

"I get your point."

"You met Mary. She's Doc Tim's nurse." Mrs. Garth laughed. "And a bit more."

"He gave me a shot."

"Tetanus booster. You ran a rusty nail into your hand. Don't show me a look. My people have been in the county a hundred years. You've had commerce with lots of them."

"Who besides your sister?"

"Mr. Wilkins at the garage. He fixed your old Jeep. And Miss Belva. She's some sort of cousin." Mrs. Garth arched her brow. "Not sure what of yours she fixed."

Theo folded his napkin and carried his dishes to the sink. "I don't think chucking Martha outdoors is going to fix her, not in a good way."

"You know where she is now?"

"In her room?"

"Talking to Miss Nadir. Martha hardly knows any real people." Mrs. Garth unplugged the percolator. "You want coffee?" Theo nodded. She filled his cup.

"Where is Mr. Garth?" Theo asked.

"I'd like to know myself. He hitched to Holcombe County to look for work and never came back. Not that I minded. We weren't together long. Trains always interested him. He might have found a railroad job."

"I hear a train every morning."

"The track along the river, my granddaddy help lay it. The company used prisoners, Black men mostly, but they weren't allowed to set off the dynamite to free out the rocks. Granddaddy did that. Later he was county clerk." She untied her apron and draped it over a chair. "What about your people—where was it?"

"Ohio."

"The missis said you came here to find a relative and Jefferson was helping you."

"Not quite. I'm trying to find out what happened to a relative. He was in the Army."

"And he was visiting here?"

"Serving. 1865."

Mrs. Garth stared at Theo. "Federal side?"

"Yes, ma'am."

She looked at the clock on the wall above the sink. "Time for my Tuesday tonic." Theo watched her take a bottle and glasses from the cupboard in the pantry. "Sherry wine. Want a taste?"

"Any good?"

"Pleases my palate, but yours is probably more sophisticated."

"Why is it special for Tuesdays?"

"Just an expression. Go on about this relative."

"His body was shipped home, except it wasn't him."

"Milo would be interested. The book he's writing is set back then, time when the war ended and folks tried to pick up the lives they had before Mr. Lincoln and all them got to fussing."

"Was there much fuss here?"

"Some, but most just wanted to be left alone. Worst was when troops from one side or the other—enforcers I think they were called—would ride around and snatch any man or boy fit to be a soldier. The person could be fifteen or fifty. One of my kin was walking to the river when a Yankee bunch spied him. He pretended to be crazy, even scooped up dirt and ate it, so they let him go."

The sherry tasted harsh, like medicine, but Theo drank his and thanked Mrs. Garth for his supper and her company. Duncan roused himself and followed Theo into the hall. Halfway to his room, he remembered the book he had left in the kitchen and turned around. He expected to find Mrs. Garth finishing the washing up, but the room was empty, and the sherry bottle was gone as well.

AFTER DINNER MILO HAD retreated to his parlor. The Victorian paintings of elaborate vases and floral bouquets, images intended to comfort those who visited the deceased when the room was the family's funeral parlor as was the custom before death became a commercial enterprise, had been sent to the attic by Chester Drew, Milo's grandfather, who took his evening meal in the parlor because his wife disapproved of his fondness for Madeira and tobacco. The bare white walls were, Milo joked, as pure and empty as his mind, which everyone knew was filled with fragments of stories and disappointment. He had married Calla at the height of his career—a best seller, his picture in the Sunday papers, first-class flights to discuss scripts and projects—followed by what he called his reunion with obscurity. His work wasn't interesting anymore. His characters dull and repetitive: quirky moonshiners, misfits, rural rowdies, lascivious preachers, who weren't nearly as remarkable as the real-life households of greedy evangelists and their spendthrift wives regularly exposed in the national press. His genre was Southern Gothic. His audience had tired of him, forgotten he was alive. Even his elderly agent was surprised that Milo continued to write anything at all. When Calla had dared to ask what Milo was working on, he answered, a love story. To which she answered, what do you know about that?

During the time Milo called his *anni mirabilium,* his wonder years, two in all, he and Calla lived in California. When his parents died, both by cancer within a month of each other, he took up residence in the Castle and made Chester's hideout into his own. Milo's desk was an oak door supported at each end by trestles that had borne the weight of family caskets. The door itself had been used to bear Confederate dead from wagons to the cemetery. Shelves filled with reference works and dictionaries had been salvaged from his father's law office. The leather couch had survived the Wrenn House, an historic brothel in Almsville, the county seat of Holcombe County, set on fire by a crazed patron who imagined himself to be the son of Toulouse-Lautrec. The woven rugs were acquired by Milo's uncle when he served in the American embassy in Turkey when Hoover was president. Milo kept whiskey and glasses in the dry sink that had belonged to an Irish ancestor. The gray Underwood typewriter had no history other than its relationship with Milo.

Mrs. Garth emerged from the closet. "Do you want to drink what you have or what I'm drinking?" he asked.

"Yours is better," she said.

They sat on the couch and emptied their glasses. Mrs. Garth sighed and welcomed Milo's hand under her skirt. Mr. Garth had been specific and quick, one place for him to be, one thing to do, and nothing else mattered. Milo (though she never spoke or whispered his Christian name) enjoyed kissing and caressing his way to what he called—with a tone of irony she thought—the portal of pleasure, which he made sure was wet and welcoming before he entered. There he stayed awhile until *spent*—a word used by earlier writers that he as well favored for such circumstances. Thereafter he sometimes napped until Mrs. Garth gently nudged him awake and reminded him that the missus would be home soon. He then knelt before the portal, inhaled its dampness, and kissed it farewell.

Mrs. Garth would disappear into the closet. Milo would pour himself another drink and contemplate his desk and its dark history and the bits and pieces of his ancestors' lives scattered about the room and consider how in him the wide scope of generations of Drews had contracted and narrowed to the county, the town, and this land. No more I go a roving, he said to himself. Martha had inherited—what to call it? Some sort of malaise? Some sort of weariness or wariness? At least he would walk the orchard or drive to Holcombe County to buy whiskey, but she would never leave the house. Unless something changed, she would grow up literate and wise in some ways, ignorant and utterly innocent in others.

He wasn't sure he trusted Theo. Like Adam, he might upset the apple cart. And Jefferson, a bastard brother with the Drew name, paid off with a substantial inheritance from their father, without claim to the family's assets. A parenthetical branch of the family's withering tree.

In the morning Nandina woke me. Tates would sleep until noon. She handed me a biscuit and what passed for coffee. I could be on my way, or I could climb the ladder and set about fixing the roof. She pointed where I would find wood and such. Tates was a sound sleeper. The noise wouldn't wake him. She stood looking down at me. Thereupon I rose, ate my biscuit, and found the ladder.

I had cut out the rotted wood and set about sawing replacements. Tates stepped from the cabin hitching up his trousers. He squinted at me like the light pained his eyes. You been here long? he asked. I said, Slept in the barn. Your missus fed me, so I owed her work and noticed your roof needed some.

He asked where I was from and where I was going. I pointed behind me. Tennessee, I said. Trout's Rangers. I have a quick mind for making up names. Never heard of them, he said, but from the color of my britches, he reckoned what side I was on. He told me he'd been drinking in Elland. He needed to explain it was the county seat, five miles east as the crow flies, a town along the river. The body of a Yankee soldier had caught in some rocks. A man who lived in a big home uphill from the courthouse stood everyone a drink at the tavern. Sort of a sendoff for the dead man's soul and one less of them walking the earth.

I asked about the body. The man from up the hill would arrange to have it properly buried. When they saw off your arm, they just throw it in a bucket with someone else's parts. At least you're alive, I said. He considered that for a moment. Have a faithful mule and a wife, he replied. I went back to work, wondering to myself why he didn't say his wife was faithful. If she was or wasn't. Or if I was wondering too much.

Noontime, Nandina and Tates carried the table outside and we shared a meal, the sun bright and warm. He appeared to be feeling better. She had told him I was a teacher. He seemed to respect that. He asked if I had ever done much planting. Corn and potatoes, I said. We discussed mules and plowing. If I wasn't in a hurry, I was welcome to sleep in the barn and have my meals. Hard to plow with one arm. He could use my help. We shook hands in a clumsy fashion, my right and his left.

He pushed away from the table and went into the cabin. Maybe you can teach me something, Nandina said, which got me to wondering again what I had wondered about before. Tates returned with a pair of old trousers. He said, Make do with these. Yours need washing.

In the barn I put on what he gave me. A few minutes later he came for the mule. Going to the Davis place, he said. He was owed money.

Wasn't long before I finished the roof. In a tub behind the cabin, Nandina had boiled my britches and drawers. When she tried to rub them clean, the drawers fell apart. I told her that most soldiers

I knew had thrown theirs away. She had heard some soldiers didn't have shoes unless they stole them from the dead. I didn't tell her how one twilight I had borrowed a field glass and watched in the distance a survivor taking the brogans from a body to wear on his own feet. I sorrowed for both men.

Nandina spread my britches on a bush to dry. She handed me a rough cloth and lye soap. The water was cool enough now for me to scrub myself. I won't be spying, she said, and disappeared into the cabin. When I was clean and dressed again, she studied me up and down, trying not to smile.

Tates returned before the rain. Nandina laid my pants on the hearth to finish drying them. We sat on the porch and watched the wind shake the blossoms on the apple tree. Saw Vesper, Tates said. Wandering like always. Nandina explained Vesper was an orphan girl. She slept in a cattle shed on Preacher Landry's property. He fed her some, but when he was riding his circuit, she stole or begged food. Harvest time Mr. Davis hired her to help him make brandy. Helped him drink it too, Nandina said. She gave Tates a look. He acted like he didn't notice.

In the morning Tates and I filed the plow sharp to open the earth. He said, Some prefer to speak a prayer for a bountiful harvest. He spat, which was what he preferred.

III

"Jefferson, I saw you drive up. What a pleasant surprise."

"Milo, white lies don't become you."

"I shall disregard that. May I offer you refreshment—coffee, tea, sarsaparilla? And why are you here?"

"To collect Theo."

"Ah, yes, 'tis Wednesday. His day to wander."

"No to refreshment."

"I suppose you shall satisfy yourself later at Dolley's."

"Probably. What are you working on?"

"This." Milo held up a book.

"Looks old," Jefferson said.

"Very. Chandler Gordon, my friend who owns a wonderful bookshop in Almsville, acquired it and thought I'd be interested." Milo pushed some papers aside and found a catalog. "He described the item as a book of notes and memoranda, small quarto, 156 lined pages, edges browned, notable wear to cover, binding loose. Name A. Provender on pasted label. You may recall that Abraham Provender was our sheriff during the conflict between the states. Chandler bought the item from a man named Brown, who claimed to have found it among some discarded volumes left curbside in Almsville. However, from Chandler's description, I suspect Mr. Brown was really Mr. Terry, the former custodian of the Mott County Library. I believe he stole the book from an archive of uncatalogued volumes that appeared to have little value other than being fragile and old."

"So what you've got is Provender's accounts?"

"Yes and no. A few pages contain entries of his personal expenses related to his work as sheriff—fees he paid out of pocket to deputies when he needed them or citizens who had information. Informants, I suppose you'd say. Charges at stables one place or another. Clothing items, like a winter coat. Meals. Hotel charge in Swain County where he went to bring back a felon wanted here. Then there are notes to himself. Questions about people and events. Observations about weather. Two things in particular stayed on his mind—the habits of a wounded farmer who seemed to favor drink, card playing, and fornication to working the soil, and the bodies of two Union soldiers, one pulled out of the river, the other found in the grass upstream."

"Was it the body of one of those men that Wells referred to in his book about the Western counties—the body laid out in a casket in the window of the furniture maker's workshop?"

"It is. Something Mr. Vos might be interested in."

"Milo, when you're not holed up writing, what are you doing?"

"Drinking. Remembering. Walking the dog. Staring out the window."

"Avoiding family and friends?"

"I have no friends."

"Martha is special. Don't neglect her."

MARTHA HAD FOUND THEO in the sunroom. "Here." She handed Theo a scrap of paper. "Daddy dropped it in the hall. Last night. He was bumping into things. Read and translate. I don't know French."

"*Je sais que le fruit tombe au vent qui le secoue*. I know that fruit falls in the wind that shakes it. *Que l'oisseau perd sa plume et la fleur son parfum.* That the bird loses its feather and the flower its fragrance. *Que la création est une grande roue.* That the creation is a great wheel. *Que ne peut se mouvoir sans écraser quelqu'un.* Which cannot move without running over something."

"Who wrote that?" Calla stood in the door, listening.

"Victor Hugo," Theo said.

"When?" Martha asked.

"Not sure, but around a hundred and fifty years ago."

"Romantic babble," Calla said. "Milo in his gloom period again. Goes with the season. The autumnal knife at his heart. Used to be he quoted Keats, 'Ode to Autumn.' Something a bit more cheerful."

Jefferson loomed in the doorway. He paid no attention to Calla but hugged Martha and waltzed her around the room.

JEFFERSON PARKED HIS BLAZER by a stone chapel near a quarry above the river. He and Theo had been walking an hour and seen several deer and, in the distance, a solitary bear.

"This land belonged to Wesley Landry," Jefferson said. He pointed downhill to a grove of willows. "There's the spring where he got his water. Your ancestor might have passed by here. Landry was a preacher with a reputation for welcoming strangers. In truth he was a whole lot more. During the war he traded information, much of which he probably made up. Both sides claimed him, and both sides used him to spy on each other. In the end it cost him. But he had a good run, especially with the ladies. He gave more than spiritual comfort to widows or wives whose husbands were away soldiering."

"Cost him how?"

"Someone shot him. Vesper might have known his identity, but she never told."

"She was...?"

"An orphan or a runaway, people think. Sixteen, maybe. She appeared and disappeared as she pleased, sometimes sleeping in Landry's barn or a shed, sometimes wherever she lay down, by herself or with company. She was literate—Landry might have taught her—smart, and a skillful sailor."

"Where were the boats?"

"Skiffs. Some in the river trade operated them. Most had sails. One day she sailed in a skiff upstream to Almsville and never came back."

"Who owns the land now?"

"Depends on who you ask. For years a distant Landry relative claimed it and paid taxes but never settled here. When tobacco became a cash crop, his son tried to farm but wasn't successful. The land is too rocky and steep. He sold to someone else, who pretty much let everything grow wild. Sometime in the 1880s a neighbor started pasturing cattle on a finger of the land. The law allows a person who uses land, otherwise unused and not expressly forbidden its use, to claim the land for himself. That's what happened to Landry's property. Same for the Burlidge farm."

Jefferson pointed in the opposite direction. "The Burlidge name first appeared in the tax roll in 1858. Your ancestor might have passed their place. It wasn't much. From what I've been able to learn from handed-down stories plus a couple of references in other county records, Mr. Burlidge was wounded in the war and couldn't milk a cow. Could lift a bottle, though. His wife did most of the work. One day she disappeared. He abandoned the farm and worked wherever whiskey or women were available to men who helped themselves to what others had left behind. A man named Clott, who owned a livery service, eventually took over the Burlidge land and got title to it. One of the Clott family began the quarry, which supplied stone for building the Castle. Milo thought of doing some research on the man. Not sure if he ever did."

The sun began to fade behind the mountains. On the way back

to the car, Jefferson stopped to photograph the shapes of trees, but it was the beauty of their shadows that attracted him.

The leaves had turned drab and dull. Dolley's was almost empty. Belva leaned over Theo's shoulder. "You boys look like you need beer and burgers."

"Bourbon," Jefferson said. "The best you got. My thirst is running high."

"Any reason?"

"The joy of living, sweetheart."

"I'll stick with beer," Theo said. "Whatever's cold and cheap. My pocketbook is running low."

"You've not been around lately. I imagine Miz Drew is cold and expensive. At least I have my memories to keep me warm. Not sure about her."

"Bring the drinks," Jefferson said. They watched Belva walk back to the bar. "Don't think she could fit into pants any tighter. Puts on quite a show."

Belva returned with Jefferson's whiskey and Theo's beer. She asked him if he'd discovered the secret ways she'd heard about. "You know," she said, "hidden passages in the Castle to sneak from one room to another."

Theo looked at Jefferson. "Are there any?"

"At least one. When Chester Drew, Milo's grandfather, was alive, he would lock himself in the parlor and no one ever saw the cook bring him roast beef and all the fatty delights the doctor warned Chester not to eat. Said they would kill him. There had to be a way the cook could do that without being seen." Jefferson sipped his drink. "The doctor was right, of course. After the funeral Milo's grandmother fired the cook."

Belva said, "*Milo's* grandparents? Weren't they yours too?"

"I was my father's mistake, not a genuine Drew," Jefferson said.

A few of the regulars began to show up. Connie had the night off. Belva got busy. Ralph brought the table a second round of drinks and took the pizza order.

"Believe in ghosts?" Jefferson asked.

"I believe people who believe in them."

"Milo said one night he was staring into space trying to remember the title of a poem by somebody—Freneau, I think—when Chester's ghost appeared, looked at Milo, shook its head in sorrow, and went away."

"Alcohol plays tricks on the dozy mind."

The mule was slow. The ground thick as clay. I ached for days. Mostly Tates watched Nandina and me plow and plant. There was some weed he was allergic to. Every spring his skin turned red and blistered. We would quit early so he could unhitch the mule and ride it to town. The doctor there could fix him a salve. Nandina and I would eat. She kept a bowl warm for him. Night before he returned. I would be in the barn, asleep in the hay until his voice woke me. He cursed the dark. He cursed the man who had wounded him. He cursed the man who doctored him. He cursed the land. He cursed the plow. He stumbled into the night to find Nandina, determined there would be a child in her yet. A boy this time.

Milo leaned away from the typewriter and stared at his whiskey, considered its amber color, its glossy keenness on the tongue. Then he drank. He said to himself a line from the Song of Solomon. "Thy navel is like a round goblet." Had Milo ever spoken it to one of his lovers? "Your waist is a mound of wheat encircled by lilies." Perhaps only to the redhaired Ruth. Any other would have laughed. Not Ruth. Sixteen, they were and parked above the river, she the high school's math prodigy, already taking classes at the college. She was not lovely, but she was lonely and eager. He had never touched a woman below the waist. She took his hand and spread her legs. He had said nothing, his brain too dazzled and stunned for speech. Oh, to have that moment back again, the pure amazement of touch and texture and smell. There was mystery too. More than he was prepared to explore. Are you going to go and leave me this way? The last words she ever spoke to him.

"What do you make of Martha?" Calla asked.

Mrs. Garth had tidied the kitchen and gone to shop at the new supermarket in the cluster of stores across the county line. Calla was watering the pots of herbs and the cyclamen on the ledge below the tall windows. Theo poured what was left of the coffee in the dented percolator into his cup.

"She needs structure."

"Can't you provide it?"

"She wanders—both in mind and body. She objects to topics or schedules. It's a bit of this, a bit of that. She nibbles, never sits for a whole meal."

"Perhaps your culinary skills are lacking. Last night, how was your burger?"

"Filling."

"And Belva?"

"What about her?"

"Theo, you're a bit sharp this morning. And please call me Calla." She moved the cyclamen to the table. "Belva has been described to me as bright and bawdy. I'd rather not have the Elland wags concocting stories about you and her and your job here and our family, which has always been a target of envy and misinformation. Understand?"

"I do."

Theo rinsed his cup and left it in the sink. Calla followed him into the hall. He started up the grand staircase and turned around. She stood at the bottom, her hand on the carved pineapple atop the mahogany newel. Her gaze was sad, as if she had more to say and he wasn't listening. He remembered reading that pineapples represented warmth and hospitality.

MARTHA PREFERRED MEETING THEO in the sunroom. She would slouch in one of the armchairs and prop her feet on a footstool while Theo sat facing her. The autumn sun warmed the room, the air fragrant from the damp earth in the glazed pots of hibiscus.

"Tell me a story," Martha said.

"There was an English king named Orfeo. One day his queen, the lovely Herodis, falls asleep in their orchard—"

"Daddy just walks Duncan in ours."

"Well, when Herodis wakes up, she says the king of the fairies visited her and demanded she live with him. She will be carried off if she doesn't."

"I don't get who *he* is, this fairy guy."

"I'll get back to that. So, she disappears. The grieving Orfeo, who is also a terrific harpist, gives up his kingdom and for ten years lives like a vagrant in the wilderness. He often sees the king of the fairies and his followers enjoying themselves. One day he sees Herodis. He follows the king's people through a cave and eventually to a splendid castle where he gains entrance, claiming to be a minstrel. The king of the fairies is so beguiled by Orfeo's playing that he allows Orfeo a reward of his choice. Of course, he asks for Herodis. Disguised, the couple return to their former kingdom. Orfeo's faithful steward recognizes Orfeo's harp, which he tells the steward he found next to a dead man. The steward, thinking the body must be his former king's, weeps. Whereupon Orfeo sheds his disguise and reveals his identity. The court is joyful. Orfeo is crowned their king again, and the kingdom's harpists write a lay in Orfeo's honor."

"What's a lay? It's nothing to do with sex, is it?"

"Not exactly. A lay is a short, rhymed story, like the one you've just heard, minus the rhyme. We talked about chivalry before. Lays are generally about chivalry and love."

"So what you said is Orpheus again, only this time with a happy ending. What's the point?"

"What's the point of the story, or why did I tell it to you?"

"Both."

"What do you imagine the story's about?"

"Love is more important than things like being king. Faithfulness, maybe. I can't imagine Daddy going out of his way to get Mother back or taking it hard if she left." Martha slouched deeper into her chair. "That's kind of too bad, isn't it?"

"Who else is faithful?"

"The steward guy. I'm not sure what he does."

"What about the king of the fairies? He couldn't have been pleased with Orfeo's choice."

"Right. He kept his word."

"I like the Orpheus story because, like many others, it exists across centuries and cultures. It's interesting because of the journey to an otherworld and return. Think of the contrasting elements of loss and recovery, wealth and poverty, and the power of art—music in this story."

"Who are the fairies?"

"Folklore beings with magic powers. They could be handsome and lovely but always dangerous. Some played tricks on people, like pixies or elves are supposed to do."

"What would you do if the king of the fairies came into my room and took me away. Would you come after me?"

"Of course."

"What if I liked the king? He might be good looking and build me a—what did you call it the other day, a bower of bliss? What if he made one of those for me and let me eat and drink what I wanted to and dress in whatever pleased me. What if he pleasured me until I couldn't see straight?"

"I'm not sure what you mean."

"What you do with that woman Mother talks about—Belva something. I know the word but promised I wouldn't say it. Daddy has some books that describe it. I'm not supposed to know about them, but sometimes when he's gone to buy his whiskey, I sneak into his parlor and read them. One has pictures. Pistil Pete told me lots of stuff. I've heard Mrs. Garth say stuff too."

"Well, if you liked the king, then you could stay, but you would probably have to learn to ride a horse and travel the hills and forests and bathe in the streams and rivers."

"If you followed me, would that mean you loved me?"

"It might."

"Do you think I'm pretty?"

"And smart."

Martha twirled a lock of her hair around her finger and stared at Theo. "Do you think my mother's pretty?"

Theo hesitated. "Yes."

"More pretty than Belva?"

"I don't make judgments like that."

"I do. You're better looking than Daddy and Jefferson. And way better than the men I watch out the window tending the lawn or fixing this and that."

"Let's talk about the poetry book I gave you."

"Don't change the subject. Tuesday nights, you know Calla meets her friends in the village?"

"Sometimes you call your mother *Calla*, sometimes you don't. Any reason?"

"*Calla* is more objective, and she wouldn't like it." Martha's fingertip traced a smile on her lips. "What I would like is you visiting my room when she's away."

"Calla wouldn't like it."

"Do you know this house has secret passages?"

"How many?"

"One I know about. Mrs. Garth uses it on Tuesdays to visit Daddy."

"If your mother's not here, why does she need a secret passage?"

"So I don't find out."

"But you did."

"I followed her. That's how I sneak into Daddy's parlor when he's away."

"You followed her…"

"I heard rustling sounds like clothes make, but I didn't see anything. I stayed back so they wouldn't see me. The air was stale and dusty. I thought I might sneeze, so I tiptoed away."

"May I?"

Theo stepped aside. Calla stepped into his room. She appeared abrupt and determined as if she had made up her mind about something. "You are happy here?" she asked. "Comfortable? Content?"

"Yes," he said.

"Chilly."

Did she mean the temperature in the room or their relationship?

"Mrs. Drew—"

"*Calla.* It will get colder."

She sat on the edge of the bed and crossed her legs at her ankles. She had on a purple cable-knit sweater, gray slacks, and black ballet shoes.

She spread her fingers and stoked the pillow. "This used to be our bed—Milo's and mine. When we slept together, not so long ago, but it feels like ages now. When the pleasure he found in a bottle pleased him more than what I was able to give him, we chose to sleep in separate rooms. The bed was too big for the room I chose. With Mrs. Garth's help, I moved it up here."

Calla sighed and lay back, her head on the pillow. The tension disappeared from her body. She inched her hand under her sweater. "Sometimes I crept up here by myself and..." Her hand slid back and forth. "*Remembered* is a way to put it."

She sat up again. "Martha said you said if fairies abducted her, you would save her."

"I don't think that's going to happen."

"Perhaps Milo's garden gnome might come alive and cause trouble. Gnomes are members of the fairy world, aren't they?"

"They are."

"What would you do, Theo, if the gnome came alive and led Martha away? Theo to the rescue?"

"Certainly."

"Once you saved her, would you marry her?"

"Wouldn't that be a requirement of the story?"

"Wouldn't passionate love making be required too?"

"I suppose so."

Calla warned herself to stop. Leave Theo alone. No teasing. Why not? "You told Martha I was pretty. If the gnome stole me away, would you be a knight in shining armor and save me?"

"I'd try."

Enough. She paid no attention. "And if you succeeded, would you cast off your shining armor and make love to me?"

"What happened to the marriage part?"

"I'm already married."

"So it wouldn't matter?"

The warning again. Calla stood up. "Not anymore," she said and left the room. Theo heard her slowly, softly descending the stairs as if each step she took required careful consideration.

I still had my briar pipe. I had cracked its stem and hollowed a reed to make a new one. No tobacco for a long time. None since my last tobacco ration. Tates said people in the county used to grow it but farmed other crops during the war to feed the soldiers. They were getting back to it now. He would find me some, though, and bring it home. He preferred cigars. The gentleman's smoke, he called them.

There was always a chore. If I wasn't repairing the barn, I was hauling rocks from the hillside to shore up the sty for the pigs or clearing trees and shrubs for a new field. Tates had in mind raising tobacco himself. Afternoons I liked to ease my back with a walk. The days were hot now, the sky hazy, the clouds high and puffy. Sultry, Nandina said. When Tates was away, she would take her lye soap and a cotton towel and go off to the spring. She would wink and say, Don't you be spying on me. I thought of the elders lusting after naked Susanna and felt ashamed.

I was never sure how much property Tates owned, but he seemed to know where the boundaries were. One he called Simple Creek, which was clear and bright and eventually flowed into the French Broad near a tavern where drovers stayed along what my map named the Holcombe Turnpike. The water was spoiled there by cattle and what Nandina called peoples' goings-on. Women and whiskey, she meant.

A man named Metcalf owned the tavern and made spirits. He needed better water and traded Tates a good horse and a bit of cash to draw from where Tates had rights to the creek. It got so that Tates was helping Metcalf so much that Nandina said Tates was Metcalf's man and his best customer. That left me the mule and, if I had thought about it, Nandina. I put Susanna out of mind. Yards away I sat on the hillside in the shade of a walnut tree and watched Nandina strip and bathe in the cold water of the spring. She turned toward me, dried herself, and took her time arranging her hair before covering herself with her clothes again.

Tates brought me tobacco and a copy of the county paper, the Lookout, which had published monthly until the second year of the war. Now it was catching up on events after the citizenry agreed the conflict had ended and neighbors might go about again without fearing someone would ambush them for supporting the wrong cause. The body found floating in the river was one story, another was a corpse discovered in tall grass near the river. The body was carried to Doctor Kitts' stable and later embalmed by a man named Duff at a cost of five dollars, which included the price of a casket. The remains, clothed again in uniform, were presently displayed in the window of Duff's furniture shop.

And *my* remains, what of them? Milo said to the part of himself that always responded with its own question, a private colloquy in which Milo asked what only he cared about and only he could answer. Your remains—what do they matter? To which he replied: Naked I came, Naked I leave the scene, Booze and words, My pastime in between. A bit of plagiarism, but a source so obscure few could identify it.

Perhaps I should have been a poet, he said and poured himself another whiskey. He heard footsteps in the hall. Glass in hand, he rose and opened the door and saw Theo.

"Ah, the lonely tutor. Pray tell, whither has gone the visionary gleam, or something like it? Do you have the correct words?"

"'Whither is fled the visionary gleam? Where is it now, the glory and the dream?'"

"How refreshing Wordsworth is still available to comfort us in our sullied hours." Milo tugged Theo's sleeve. "Come. I have spirits and an empty glass. We can discuss the matter."

Theo took the glass Milo handed him. "The couch is more comfortable than the chair," he said. He wheeled his own chair away from his desk. "I've spied you coming and going. I apologize for keeping my distance. I used to be sociable. Now I hide and try to tap a few words onto paper from a brain that is almost tapped out. I feel years older than I am. My agent, if he thinks of me at all, thinks I'm not worth even a phone call or a cheery note." Milo laughed. "I'm not noteworthy anymore. The glory and the dream kaput." Milo tasted his whiskey. "Any progress with Martha?"

"She's bright and full of questions."

"About what?"

"Today, God."

"Oh, my. I suppose old Wordsworth would tell her to get out of the house and sniff around a bit, check out the dirt and the daffodils. Not the season for those. Perhaps autumnal mums would do. What are you filling her head with?"

"Historical references. Saint Augustine, et cetera."

"Helpful?"

"Not at all."

"Perhaps that's the explanation you seek—not at all. Tell her God is made up. She'll ask why, and you'll say, because we need him. Or her. The Greeks and Romans had their mythology. We have ours."

"I'd rather change the subject."

"Ours now, or hers?"

"I'm not qualified to talk about God."

"Do you have an opinion?"

"Yes."

"*No* would be an even shorter answer."

"It's not mine."

Milo emptied his glass. "Well—what's life like in town? I hear you and Jefferson enjoy beverages at Dolley's."

"We do."

"I'm not sure it was smart of our citizens to legalize public establishments serving liquor. They are required to sell what the state sells them. Some of our local providers are going to be out of business. Know what that means?"

"Tell me."

"Those fellows will turn to raising dope. And that will provoke the Feds to take to the skies, fly those noisy propeller relics they have, buzz them low over the fields looking for marijuana crops and scaring kine in the process. Farmers will raise hell. Pretty soon voters will want things to be like they used to be." Milo replenished his glass. "Must admit, though, what I buy from the state is superior to the local product. One day Mott County will have a state store, and I won't need to drive to Holcombe County to buy my supplies."

Milo held out the bottle to Theo. "Connie Yancey works at Dolley's, doesn't she?"

"She talks about you."

"She's a good writer. The college should have treated her better."

Theo topped off his glass and passed the bottle to Milo, who set it on his desk. "Ralph Bunch—you know, who owns Dolley's—he's Connie's father, but Mrs. Bunch isn't Connie's mother. Ralph has a son—Jordan—Connie's half-brother, like Jefferson is mine. Their being together—Jefferson and Connie—seems inevitable somehow, as if they share a parallel heritage that draws them together. They think it's sexual attraction, but it's deeper than that. Forces we can't identify or control work through us. Atoms of fate, the ancients said. Now, I suppose, the DNA of fate is more appropriate." Milo scratched his chin. "The DNA of destiny—has a nice ring to it. Don't you agree?"

Milo drank more whiskey. "Sorry. After nine, I'm never focused or coherent. My mind wanders." He drank again. "The atoms controlling Martha—wondering what they are keeps me awake."

MARTHA'S ROOMS ON THE second floor were not girly. The furniture and décor were one thing Calla and Miss Nadir agreed on. No dolls, no cuddly animals. No preponderance of pinks. No ruffles. Only the basics. Room 1: Bookshelves, chairs, tables, lamps, desk, rugs. 2: Dressing table, chair, bureau, closets, mirrors. 3: Four-poster bed, night table, blanket chest, rugs, chair, armoire. The bathroom was dark wood, white toilet, sink, tub, the shower a curve of fretted chrome. Spiders had woven webs under the flaking radiator.

Martha liked the way the tan beanbag chair shaped itself to accommodate her. She leaned back, raised her legs, and hugged them to her chest.

Miss Nadir didn't approve. "You mustn't show so much of yourself," she said.

"Then what's the point of pretty underwear?" Martha asked.

"For you to feel the pleasure of dressing in pretty things," Miss Nadir replied. "The best pleasures are secret ones."

No secret, however, that Martha's underwear was selected by Calla's sister, for whom buying gifts for her niece was not only an opportunity to re-imagine her own younger self as a more alluring and flirtatious than she had been but also to preserve the tenuous bond of family forever frayed by sniping and recriminations after the loss of the family's position and property.

Martha thought a moment. Miss Nadir was shifty, always moving about, both in mind and body. She popped up anywhere, often inconveniently. Martha stretched out her legs and tapped her heels together. "Miss Nadir, what would you tell a writer if no one read what he wrote? Would you tell him he should feel satisfied knowing he had written something he wanted to write, that having a readership isn't part of the deal?"

"Authorship is not in my purview," Miss Nadir said, "though I believe many eyes should not have gazed upon much your father has written. Too sordid, too sensual."

"Too many people straying impassioned in the littering leaves?" Martha asked.

"I know you're quoting someone, but I don't know who."

"Me either. A bit of something I remember Theo reciting recently."

"Be on your guard. Theo might cause you to stray, like that boy the college sent over."

"Would Theo like to stray with me, you think?"

"I'm sure of it."

"Mrs. Garth said I might like it. She does a bit of it herself."

"Who would be interested in her? She smells of pots and pans."

"Milo perhaps?"

"He must be desperate. Men get that way."

"He's sad."

"Too much drink will do that. A fly buzzed at the window and fell onto the sill. Have you observed Mrs. Garth and Mr. Milo together? I trailed her through the secret corridor from the kitchen to Daddy's parlor."

"You're making that up."

"You know I never make things up."

NOON THE NEXT DAY Calla was leaving the Laurel when Dr. Tim was entering it. "Treating myself to salty ham and red-eye gravy." He winked. "Side order of hush puppies."

"Doesn't sound healthy," Calla said.

"That's the point." He studied Calla's face. "You appear—"

"What?"

"You tell me."

"Milo's being his usually difficult self, and Martha carries on long conversations with people she makes up and hardly speaks to me. The other night I dreamed I drugged her and locked her outside."

"Then what happened?"

"I woke up, drank some water, and went back to bed."

"And?"

"I relaxed myself and fell asleep."

"You relaxed yourself how?"

"You know what I mean."

"Have you considered a lover?"

Two in ten years. Calla congratulated herself on her successful secrecy, quite an accomplishment in a small community like Elland. She gave thanks for the complicity of her bridge companions. "Are you volunteering? I'm sure Wilfred Stock has a room available."

"I'm serious."

"You believe sex with someone other than myself would make me a new woman?"

"A different one."

"A kinder, sweeter Calla? You know callas are lilies? They come in several colors. Photographers favor white. Would you have me red, full of passion?"

"How do you see yourself?"

"Faded. Definitely faded."

"Are you jealous of Martha?"

"What?"

"Perhaps I mean *envious*. The difference always confuses me."

"Make your point. Your diagnosis."

"She's the white lily, but you've detected her inclination toward red."

"Perhaps one of her imaginary companions will satisfy her."

"Your dream, when you locked her out of the house—it was snowing, wasn't it?"

"Why would you think that?"

"Deadly weather for lilies." He started to push the door and turned around. "By the way, you're due for a pneumonia shot."

"Doctor Tim, sometimes your words sting more than your needles."

IV

I had made space for myself in one of the stalls: nailed boards together for a table, packed straw for a bed, whittled pegs to hang my clothes, the few I had. Nandina provided a chipped basin for water to wash with and a tin cup to drink from.

I took off my clothes, wet from an all-day rain, and started to put on dry ones that Tates had found for me in town. I suspected he acquired them at Duff's. Nandina said he took clothes from the dead, undressed the bodies before he nailed shut their coffins. God had brought them naked into this world, why should he object to their leaving it that way?

Tates was away again. I had not heard Nandina enter the barn. Her voice surprised me. I spun around, holding my britches in front of me. She said, Let us consider the situation. You have seen plenty of me, have you not? I assented I had. Do you find me to your liking? she asked. I assented I did. Tates wanted a child, a boy this time. She was weary of his attempts. His seed was not productive now. She would be forever in my debt if mine were.

She approached me. You are blushing and I am not, she said. She reached for my arm and dismissed my defense and fingered what I had concealed. It responded to such freedom most eagerly. She cast off her clothes. Her skin smelled sweet, like the tangles of honeysuckle growing near the spring. She took my hand and brought it where she liked. Rain drummed on the roof, muffling our cadences of pleasure.

"I Fall to Pieces over You" was playing on the Wurlitzer. Connie brought Theo's beer and Jefferson's whiskey. "Ralph has a stash of local stuff," she said, "if you're interested."

Jefferson held up his glass. "I prefer my spirits to have a bit of color and age."

"That's what my daddy used to say about the female company he kept. Theo, what about you, who are you keeping company with?"

"I haven't been going out much."

"Miss Martha's too young for you, and Miss Calla—she's sort of bitchy and dried up."

"She mellows when you know her."

"And do you?"

"I'm trying too."

"Tell Milo I miss him."

"Write something and I'll pass it on."

"I'd rather take it to him myself."

"He'd like that," Jefferson said.

"Don't think Calla would." Connie wiped an empty table and walked back to the bar.

"Tell me about the body in the window," Theo said.

"It's true, at least Wells thought so. A man named Duff made caskets in his furniture shop and learned embalming. Not sure how lucrative it was. Lots of folks buried their own on their own land. Sometimes the graves were marked, sometimes they weren't. In time, weather wore away the markers, or they went missing, or folks didn't know what they were because they were just flat rocks like you find lying in a field and weren't chiseled with names or dates. Been occasions when property changed hands and the new owner plowed up bones he didn't know were there."

Jefferson glanced at the Wurlitzer. Hank Williams was asking why he couldn't free his lover's doubtful mind and melt her cold, cold heart.

"So this Duff lived above the shop, which was a place of good size near the river. The building no longer exists. The Farm Bureau insurance office sits there now. Anyway, Duff decided to advertise, at least provoke interest, by embalming the body of a man found upriver and arranging the remains in a casket displayed in the front parlor window."

"A soldier?"

"His pants, belt, and buckle were Union. The jacket found nearby was Union too. So was his canteen. There weren't any ration cards and few personal items. Thing is, according to the stories Wells heard, Duff said the jacket didn't fit the body, sleeves too short. Duff wasn't sure the body and the jacket belonged to the same man. Duff had to provide a jacket that fit him. There was a shirt found too. Hadn't been worn much. It had long sleeves."

Jefferson finished his whiskey. "Wells conjectured that Duff may have had other purpose than advertising by displaying the body. The dead man had been shot—in the back. Murdered, most likely. Duff may have thought by putting the victim where anyone could see him, someone might recognize the body. There might be profit reuniting the dead man with his family."

Jefferson held up his empty glass, and Connie brought him a full one. "You're supposed to drink and be merry," she said.

"I am," Jefferson said.

"You don't look it. The two of you always appear to be having a solemn conversation, like you're plotting something sinister."

"Why don't you write a story about it?" Theo said.

"Oh, I been doing that, but all in my head. You're planning to kidnap Miss Martha—the whole bunch of you, including her mother. It's how finally you get Martha out of the house. You plan to take her to a trailer somewhere in the woods. Not sure what happens next, but at some point, Theo and Martha have feelings for each other." Connie stared at Theo. "Maybe she does already."

"She plays games," Theo said. "Sits in ways to show off a bit too much of herself."

"How do you react?"

"I try not to notice."

"You do, though."

"It doesn't mean anything."

"It does to her. She's teasing you. Trying out what works or doesn't. A game, but a serious one—for her."

"You have other customers."

"Hint taken," Connie said and walked away.

"Touched a nerve?" Jefferson asked.

"Let's call it a night," Theo said.

THE KITCHEN LIGHTS WERE on. Theo expected to encounter Mrs. Garth, but Calla, barefoot and wearing a pale blue robe, was staring out the window. "Supposed to be a meteor shower. Don't see anything."

"Too cloudy," Theo said.

"You been with Jefferson, drinking?"

"Anything wrong with that?"

"Theo, I'm not criticizing." Her voice—lately Theo thought it was softer, kinder, more Southern. "Merely inquiring. Now I'm here, a bit of something spiritual might help me sleep."

She walked to the pantry, opened a cupboard, reached behind rolls of paper towels, and took down a bottle. "Mrs. Garth's stash." Calla poured two glasses.

They lingered by the window. She said, "When I was in high school, a neighbor owned a plane, Piper Cub, I think. Sometimes he took me flying. Sometimes I climbed out of my seat and squeezed into his so he could teach me to steer."

"Sounds awkward."

"Not for what he had in mind."

"I suppose you learned a lot."

"He said I was a natural."

She finished her drink. Theo had scarcely touched his. "May I?" She took his glass and poured half his sherry into hers. After she drank that, she set her glass on the sill and confronted her reflection in the window as if there was a choice and a decision needed making. She turned toward Theo. "Would the gentleman be embarrassed if I asked him to kiss me?"

"Are you asking?"

"I believe I am," she said and lifted her face to his.

"Nice." She pressed her thumb against his lips. "When you're finished, put the bottle away and turn off the lights."

Theo looked outside to see if the garden gnome was where it was supposed to be.

"Seventeen tomorrow. Who is coming to your party?" Theo asked.

"Miss Nadir, Miss Grimm, and I are celebrating privately. Calla plans a fête or some such with the two of you. Daddy will attend—if he remembers."

"Presents?"

"Shall you have one for me?"

"Of course."

"Already picked out? Wrapped in tissue paper and pink ribbon?"

"Brown paper."

"Oh, is it something naughty?"

"Don't think so."

"A book, I bet."

"Could be. Is there one you especially want?"

"Yes, a narrative of anatomy."

"Gray's?"

"Not familiar with him. No, what I'm thinking of involves letters."

"Fiction?"

"There's truth in it."

"That's true of most fiction."

"I suppose."

"Another clue?"

"It's an...*epistolary*—I think that's the right word—epistolary novel. Eighteenth century. Letters from a woman. Something you might read under the covers. Lots of legal issues. Its publication was a hard hill to climb. That's another clue."

"*Fanny Hill*?"

"Précisément. Daddy has his own copy. When he was away on one of his buying trips, I found it. I'd like my own copy."

"Why?"

"I might learn something."

"You might."

"Well?"

"Sorry, but you'll have to settle for something a bit chillier and poetic."

"Is that a clue?"

"Possibly."

"Was the author born in San Francisco?"

"You're way ahead of me."

"Frost. I like him. He's so rhymey. I'll act surprised."

"Seriously, will being seventeen mean anything to you?"

"I wanted to invite Pistil Pete to my party. Calla objected."

"You haven't answered my question."

"Think about it. I have."

Martha slouched further into her chair. Theo said, "I forgot what we were supposed to be talking about."

"Polk and Western expansion. He was almost a local boy."

"Besides where he was born, what else do you know about him?"

"He sent a guy named Taylor to get Texas from the Mexicans. He did such a good job he became president. He was supposed to be inaugurated on a Sunday, but he wouldn't do it on the Sabbath. Someone had to be temp president for a day."

"Something I didn't know."

"Point for my side, Smartie." Martha sighed. "Something else you don't know—what I want you to give me for a birthday."

"Other than *Fanny Hill*?"

"Forget her. A kiss. A real kiss. Deep and wet, like Pistil Pete said they should be. I saw you with Calla. I can do better. Can you?"

"You shouldn't spy on people."

"You haven't answered *my* question."

"Only if we do it outside."

Martha waved at the window. "Out there, you mean?"

"Yes, out there."

"You shouldn't trick people. It's beneath you."

Summer was hot. More and more I did the farming. Some animals were after the corn. Coons, maybe. Nandina hoped it was deer. During the war, soldiers had shot most of them and the turkeys. At night a bear would tear up a bush or break branches off an apple tree that Nandina cherished. The bear was marking his territory, Tates said. He gave me a hard look, like Nandina was his territory and I best be careful. The baby would be born when the sky was holding the light longer again.

Tates talked about town and seeing the body in a casket in the furniture maker's window. Wasn't a Yankee soldier like people thought he was. A traveler recognized the man, said his name was Grundy. His people lived in Burke County and owned mines. He had served the South and written home that he was investigating the possibility of finding gold in Mott County creeks and streams. Slaves worked his family's mines. They wanted wages now. He was bitter about losing the war. He drank and had a temper.

Provender was the name of the Mott County sheriff. According to him, Grundy being who he was and shot in the back, and the other man pulled from the river, a knife wound in his gut, it was like the two men were facing each other. Provender suspicioned someone else was there.

Tates asked if I had any opinion. Wasn't my business, I said, and asked what sort of man Provender was. Fair, Tates thought. The sheriff's leg had never healed straight from a fall from a tree when he was young. That kept him out of the war. He hadn't favored one side or the other, at least no one had heard him tell if he did. He maintained order when feelings ran high. He came down hard on a man who shot up the courthouse because the mayor wouldn't fly a Confederate flag or any flag at all.

Tates brought me more tobacco and a shirt. Mine was so full of holes and tears. The new one didn't fit. My arms weren't as long as he reckoned they were. Wear it with the sleeves rolled up, he said. Next time in town he would find another.

He suggested I go with him. The days were shorter now. Cold before you knew it. I'd need more than a shirt. I thought of the Enfield and if I could find my way to where I had hidden it. I told Tates I wasn't sure I would stay much longer. He said he wanted my help chopping the corn and shocking it. Then there was butchering and salting the hog meat. He would pay for what I needed to keep warm. A trip to town would do me good, he said. I appeared worried all the time. A taste of whiskey would cheer me up. He knew a woman who could make me smile all over. Nandina said from the smell on him he knew more than one.

I promised to think on things. I blamed myself for not throwing the Enfield into the river and leaving my caps and cartridge pouch. I missed my Bible too. I recalled Albert had borrowed it and whoever found his pack had it. I suppose there was some hidden Christian message there related to my indifference to keeping my Bible close at hand, but I was unwilling to work out the meaning.

JEFFERSON BROUGHT MARTHA A harmonica. It came in a box with a folded sheet of instructions how to play simple tunes. "'Old Black Joe,' one of my favorites," she said and closed the box. Theo doubted she would open it again. His edition of Frost's poems was better received.

They sat around the table in the dining room, bright angles of afternoon sun across the floor, the wide pine boards stained by human carelessness and scarred by the bootheels of time, Milo was fond of saying as if he were a melancholy docent leading a gaggle of tourists. Mrs. Garth had the day off. Martha said Miss Nadir was feeling poorly and sent her regrets. Miss Grimm planned events but never attended them.

Martha wore a white blouse, black leggings, and beaded moccasins. Theo imagined Calla's body naked under her bright caftan. She looked at him and raised an eyebrow as if she sensed what he was thinking and wished to tease him it might be so.

Calla's present came in a box as well. Its blue velvet, its monogram stitched with gold thread, signified tradition and wealth. The moment required silence, attention, and respect. If Calla expected Martha to hold her breath, she did not. "Pearls," she said as if to talking to herself and stared at them uncertain whether to touch them and by doing so acknowledging her place in a worn-out aristocracy or to push them aside as if so overcome with surprise and gratitude she had no words to express it.

"Your grandmother's," Calla said. They were natural and not cultivated and had been worn at Wilson's inauguration. Martha mumbled she bet Old Black Joe wasn't invited. Everyone pretended not to hear her.

Milo slid his present down the table to Martha sitting at the opposite end. She untied the green bow, unfolded the silver paper, studied the book, then held it up. Everyone at the table except Theo had seen the cover many times—*Thatch* (in red caps against a dark blue background), a novel by Milo Drew (in red script, lower right).

Martha opened to the inscription on the half-title page—TO MARTHA, DAUGHTER BELOVED—and held up the book again.

"First edition," Jefferson said, because someone had to say something.

Milo rose from the table. Theo followed him into the hall. "Are you all right?"

Milo took out a handkerchief and wiped his cheek. "Absolutely pathetic," he said, "but I just want her to read something I wrote."

"She will," Theo said, although he wasn't convinced of it.

When they sat down again, Jefferson was at the sideboard opening one of the two bottles of Champagne waiting on the Sheffield tray by the urns of bittersweet. He moved around the table, filling glasses—Martha's half full.

"To Martha," everyone said and raised their glasses. Martha raised hers and touched the wine with the tip of her tongue. A sip next time, then a deep drink and a sigh as if something had been settled. By now Milo's glass was almost empty.

JEFFERSON HAD GONE HOME. Milo had returned to his parlor. Sleepy from Champagne, Martha had gone to bed. Theo helped Calla wash and dry the Sèvres plates and the Webb goblets that she had chosen in Martha's honor.

He followed Calla upstairs. She shut her bedroom door. Hands at her sides, she stood in front of the long mirror in its gilt frame and studied the reflection of Theo behind her, trying to interpret his gaze before he either offered to help her lift the caftan up and over her head or merely watched her do it as if he had paid to have her and watching was part of getting his money's worth.

The meeting in the kitchen, the kiss asked for and received, brief but nice. Never let a boy know how much you want him was her mother's advice on Calla's seventeenth birthday. "Yours if you want me," she said as if it didn't matter.

Theo stepped forward and undid the ribbon, freeing Calla's tawny hair to cover her cheeks, until he pulled it back and kissed her neck. She turned and kissed his mouth and felt him slide his hands over her hips and take hold of the caftan. "Now you," she said and loosened his belt and reached into his warmth, the shape of him swelling in her hand.

Their bodies pressed the chill out of the sheets and tangled their smells into them. Surprise. Exclamations. Pleasure. Sighs. Then the languid rearrangements and drift into sleep.

When Calla opened her eyes, Theo was staring at the ceiling. "Regrets?" she asked.

"Only wondering where we go from here."

If Dr. Tim was right and fulfilling sex would soften her, "I stay, you leave" didn't hit the right note, but she said it anyway.

"That's not what I meant."

She kissed her fingertip and pressed it to Theo's lips. "You know where to find me," she said. "Just be discreet. Milo wouldn't care, but Martha would ask questions, and I wouldn't have answers."

THEO DRESSED AND COAXED Duncan to walk with him. Clouds filled the sky. Duncan limped toward the orchard. Theo followed, trying to sort out his feelings. Yours if you want me, Calla had said. Was the afternoon a seldom thing after too much wine, or something more? What was he to her? What could he ever be besides a pleasant interruption? She had her life. He stared at the Castle. He had no life there. Even if Milo would not object, Theo felt he had betrayed him and would do so again. He had feelings for Calla, though he could not sort out what they were. Nor could he know what hers were other than needing the comfort of touch, which as much as giving her pleasure affirmed her identity, assured her that her younger self, the Tidewater debutante, had not aged away.

Had he not betrayed Martha too? Connie was right. Martha was playing him, exposing herself in languid poses, arousing him, or at least confusing him with the ambiguity of appearing to propose a willingness to explore the possibilities of arousal and its consequences. To refuse her flirtations by entering a relationship with Calla would wound Martha deeply. Theo was not hired to tutor her in disappointment and rejection.

And Belva—what were they to each other? It was all too much to sort out, which assumed he was in control of the situation and the person capable of sorting it out. But am I? he wondered. Calla could get along very well without him. So could Belva. He wasn't so sure about Martha.

Rain tapped the leaves. Duncan turned around. In Ohio the trees would be bare. His mother had walked him to his Jeep. He had said, I hope it gets me there. She had said, I hope you find someone who makes you happy.

THEO AND JEFFERSON AGREED Miss Tripp would enjoy an evening at Dolley's. Ralph served them himself, pleased to have the company of a professor—a PhD in fact—to give the establishment a little class. If Miss Tripp—Louise—felt concern that a talented student like Connie was waitressing in a bar, she showed no signs of it. She cheerfully inquired if Connie might be interested in reapplying to the college and finishing her degree. Connie replied she would give the matter some thought. Everyone knew she would not.

After speculations about the severity of the approaching winter as augured by woolly worms, the health of the college as predicted by the latest enrollment figures, and state politics as affected by redistricting, Jefferson asked Louise about Pistil Pete. She knew him as Peter Dillingham, scion of a wealthy Charlotte family, which like many families viewed the school as a safe place to park a son or daughter whose academic achievements were well below their capabilities in hopes that the small institution tucked away in the mountains would provide their underachievers with enough college credits to make them employable in some reputable occupation that paid well.

"Scion and stud," Louise said. What Peter lacked in scholarship his A-plus social life made up for.

Did he have a car? Not merely a car, but a Mercedes. Used, of course, but probably the only one in the county.

Jefferson rather off-handedly mentioned Peter's attraction to Martha and hers to him. Louise suggested that one night Jefferson or Theo might sneak Peter into the Castle and let nature take its course. Just the opposite, Jefferson said. The point was to get Martha out, not Peter in. Some jokes about ins and outs followed.

Louise noted the porte-cochere. It was outside the Castle, but not by much. A couple of steps from the front door and Martha could pop into the Mercedes and feel she wasn't really outside at all. They agreed that Peter would probably drive somewhere secluded, park and, as mentioned before, let nature take its course. Then Martha would be overcome with sensory gratification and want to go home where she felt safe and could sort out the new sensations and perceptions that assaulted her. She was not a slow learner—only a cautious one.

After another round of drinks, they agreed Martha would not step an inch out of the house for Peter or anyone else unless something drove her to it and that would not be Peter and his Mercedes.

MARTHA DRIED HERSELF AND wrapped the towel around her waist. The radiator clanked and hissed, but at least her dressing room was warm. Do try them on, Miss Nadir said. Why not, Martha thought and lifted the pearls from their box. They were yellowish like fading gardenias and felt cool and dry against her skin. She reached behind her neck, struggling with the clasp. The towel opened and fell around her feet. What would Theo make of her? she wondered. Her breasts, would they spellbind him? Her friend Annabet had liked them. Or her slender hips? Her pubis, what, exactly, was its attraction? It seemed rather ordinary to her. When Calla had pointed to it and explained what-was-what of female anatomy, or Dr. Tim had examined her on one of his routine house calls, neither had spoken of anything out of the ordinary. Only Pistil Pete had called attention to shapes and touch and hinted at exquisite pleasures, some she had read about in Mistress Hill's quaint adventures.

At it again, are we? Miss Nadir commented. Martha's fingers withdrew from her warm breast and closed around the cold clasp. She laid the pearls to rest in their velvet lining. Once hadn't they been living things? Or merely irritating visitors? So was Theo lately, distracted as if something or someone had called him away and he had lost interest in what he had been doing.

V

Noble Davis was a tall, stern man who rode a black horse that backed away when I tried to stroke it. You're not familiar to him, Davis said. He inquired where I was from. East, I answered. He appeared to consider that, all the time astride his black stallion that would not hold still but shook its head while circling me like I was some sort of exhibit that the rider was appraising and giving mind to buying.

Finally, he dismounted. He knew Tates was away again. Whiskey has its hold on him, Davis said. Women and gambling too. A shawl over her shoulder to keep off the October chill, Nandina stood at the cabin door, wiping her hands on her apron while she watched us. She had said before she had no fondness for the man.

Davis said, You hear of Vesper? I call her a woman though she be not much older than a girl. Sixteen or seventeen, I reckon. Carries on sometimes like she was eleven or twelve. Belligerent. Tates mentioned her, I answered. A wild one, Davis said. He knew as fact she wanted a child and had lain with Tates. So had others. From the evidence as

Davis counted it, Tates was incapable of fathering one. I mentioned Hester. Tates was always fond of drink. Davis doubted that Tates knew that when he was in town, a man on furlough named Bentley, who had courted Nandina before the war, rode over a time or two and stayed awhile. Davis let me draw my own conclusion. What happened to Bentley? I asked. A mini ball took him down, Davis said. Later I would understand Vesper's wish for a child was more Davis's than hers, and a boy would most certainly be to her profit.

I pointed over my shoulder in Nandina's direction. Davis said, Son, I can't swear to it, but I believe Miz Nandina's condition is your doing. Tates thinks otherwise, I said. A blessing for you he does, Davis replied. If the offspring favors your character, a blessing for Miz Nandina too.

The horse snorted and stomped. Davis held the reins tight. What then is our business? I asked. I will pay you to lie with Vesper, Davis said. On her roaming she had seen me and approved. Her body told her I would succeed where others had not.

And when would I do this? I asked. Davis turned and scanned the distance. Can't see where, but she's watching us, he said. Out there in the shadows. She's a spooky one. A wraith almost. More spirit than flesh, though the body she has is mighty tempting.

If so, I said, why not you? Davis affirmed he was sixty. His manhood was tentative. What seed he might provide would be withered and wasted.

Nandina stepped inside. Perhaps she was chilled. Perhaps she savvied what Davis was offering and didn't want to know how I would answer. He took out a purse of dollars and handed it to me. Help Tates with the butchering, then leave the county. You will need money to travel. I took the money. He said, Vesper knows your habits. Have your supper. She will find you.

He fitted his boot into the stirrup and swung himself onto the saddle. The horse glared at me and flared its nostrils. Davis's expression was earnest, concerned. He said, You told of serving in Trout's Rangers. There was a Tuttle, no Trout. Weren't called Rangers either. Tuttle's Raiders.

The horse spun around again. Davis calmed it. He said, A body folks in town thought wasn't ours is. Wouldn't surprise me there are men among us who might claim to have served those they had not. The truth will catch them out.

And what has such speculation to do with me? I inquired. Davis replied, A night when winter is setting in and Tates suggests a trip to town and sharing whiskey would warm your mood, I caution you to be careful. December you can expect snow here. Leave before anyone can track you.

"'The long day wanes,'" Milo uttered as he stumbled down the hall. In fact, the day had long since waned. Almost midnight. He paused by a window and pressed his forehead against the leaded glass. "'The slow moon climbs.'" He looked away and saw Theo ahead of him. "'The deep rolls round with many voices.'" He clutched Theo's arm. "Can't you hear them?"

"Faintly," Theo said.

Milo gripped Theo's shoulder to steady himself. "What progress with your young scholar?"

"French interests her."

"What's about the great outdoors? Any progress there?"

"Not so far."

Milo wavered and Theo guided him to a chair by a table under a framed Currier and Ives lithograph of a steamboat on the moonlit Mississippi. "That boy from the college, he wanted to…"

"Seduce her?"

"Your verb, not mine. Chosen to suggest patience and skill, I suppose." Milo shut his eyes, then opened them. "Whereas mine would imply crudeness. Force." Milo gritted his teeth. "*Fuck*. The brutal Germanic," he rasped. His eyes closed again. "What about you, my young friend? What are your feelings? I know she's tempted you."

"The world is full of temptations."

Milo's eyes were open now. "*C'est des conneries* as the French say. Bullshit. Answer the question."

"She has a lovely mind."

"You can't fuck a mind, just mess with it."

"I wouldn't be so sure about that."

"I'm damn sure the callow Mr. Dillingham had other plans, but Calla got in the way. Fired his ass. I was not consulted."

"What are you saying?"

"I was on Romeo's side."

"Dillingham as Romeo?"

"Why not? Many have played the part."

"Martha as Juliet? Dillingham mouthing lovely poetry about light breaking or teaching torches to burn bright?"

"I think Dillingham had other mouthing to do." Milo chucked. "And I, dear Theo, must hie myself to bed." Theo helped Milo up from the chair. "What about you? What midnight oil are you burning?"

"Couldn't sleep."

"You had the flush of satisfaction upon your face."

"Did I?"

Milo sniggered. "Are you messing with my mind? Or could it be…" He leaned to sniff Theo's skin and lost his balance. Theo steadied him. "I'll mess with yours. I will feel a financial obliation…"—he spoke slowly—"ob-li-ga-tion if you…well, you decide." He waved his hand as if clearing the air.

"Want me to go with you?" Theo asked.

"This old horse knows the way," Milo answered.

THE SUNROOM WAS CHEERLESS and cold. Mrs. Garth had lit a morning fire in the library's fireplace. Martha slumped in her chair, Theo opposite her. Frost melted in an edge of the window. Conley, the arthritic gardener, was outside raking leaves.

"What's the French word for cake?"

"Gâteau," Theo said.

Martha slouched deeper. No sweater and leggings today, but a jumper and plaid skirt her aunt had sent from Scotland. "Did Marie Antoinette really say, 'let them eat cake?'"

"Not sure."

Martha pulled her collar up to her chin as if hiding a smile. "Did she wear underpants?"

"Why do you ask?"

Martha flicked up her skirt. "I bet mine are prettier." Theo looked away. "Did I embarrass you?"

"Not really."

"I'll try again."

"Don't."

"I miss Pistil Pete."

"What if he came to see you?"

"Calla wouldn't let him in."

"What if he parked so close to the house that one step and you would be out the door and into his car?"

"Hmm."

"Did he kiss you?"

"I kissed him. I learned from Annabet."

"Is she a friend of Miss Nadir or Miss Grimm?"

"Annabet lived in town. She used to come here and spend time with me. We practiced kissing together. Sometimes she spent the night. Her family moved to Oregon."

"Do you miss her?"

"Not as much as Pete."

"Let's talk about the French Revolution. What do you think was going on?"

The fire puffed. Sparks popped across the hearth. "On cold nights Annabet would get into bed with me."

"Annabet isn't who we're here to talk about."

"I'm messing with your mind."

"What exactly does that mean?"

"What did it mean last night? I heard you and Daddy talking in the hall."

"You should have been asleep."

"So should you. Men get sleepy after sex."

"According to Annabet?"

"*Mais oui.*"

"*Avec qui ai-je couché*? Who did I have sex with?"

"*With whom*, if you please."

"The *answer*, if you please."

Martha laughed. "I'm teasing. Perhaps Mrs. Garth has made herself available. Daddy has been a disappointment lately. She talks to herself. 'Sleepy time down south' was how she put it. I think I know what she meant. Mistress Hill referred to the condition, one not uncommon in older men. Care to comment?"

"You realize Hill's memories were written by a man."

"Cleland, was it? Bet he earned a few bob for the publisher."

"And jail time for himself."

"At least he had his imagination to keep him company. What do you have to pass the hours?"

"I roam at night like you do."

"We might bump into each other."

"Then what?"

"You decide. You have a good imagination."

"Miss Nadir would have to approve."

"Don't spoil things."

Tates had no time for supper. He needed to attend a meeting in town. Come butchering season, salt would be in short supply again. Creating scarcities was one of the devious ways the government in Washington was inflicting further pain upon those who had opposed it. Instead of releasing salt to help the vanquished, the government was rubbing it into their wounds.

Tates missed a fine stew—a mix-up, Nandina called it. Rabbit, mushrooms, potatoes, with seasoning she made from the fruit and berries of black gum, hydrangea, and something he knew by its Cherokee name, koksagi. Dark when we ate the pie she had baked from the apples she'd been saving. I was sorry to bid her goodnight. I saw sorrow in her expression as well. She sighed as if to tell me to get about whatever Mr. Davis had ridden out of his way to speak to me about.

The bobcat was hunting again. We were accustomed to passing each other in the night. It eyed me with haughty disregard. Vesper was lying in the hay. She had cast aside her shawl and a canvas bag with a strap that looped over her shoulder. She wore a wool shirt and rough trousers. You took your time, she said. Any hurry? I asked. Depends on how we take to each other, she answered. She lifted a bottle from her bag and offered me a drink. Brandy Mr. Davis made. Didn't burn the throat like what Tates brought from town. I passed the bottle to her. She took a deep swallow. Her hair was tangled with hay from where she had been lying.

You made children before? she asked. No, I told her. She smiled. Mr. Davis thinks otherwise. He can think what he wants, I said. What do you think of me? she asked. Barns were always catching fire. Nandina didn't want me to have a candle or a lantern. Despite the gloom Vesper and I could see each well enough. I've glimpsed you before, I said. Way off. She handed me the bottle and undid her shirt and pulled it back. Up close, what's your judgment? You are nicely formed, I said. She cursed and said, You speak like Preacher Landry. His member was puny. Pull down your britches. Let's see what you got.

I did. She studied me and nodded her approval.

Let's get about the Adam-and-Eve thing, she said. I spread a blanket. She pulled off her trousers but kept her shirt on because the dust prickled her back. We did it once, emptied the bottle, and did it again. You seemed to like what you were doing, she said. That's a good sign. Means I'll have a boy.

She asked what I was called. Maybe she would name the boy after me. Plymm, I told her. Mr. Plymm or Plymm something? Just Plymm, I said and closed my eyes. When I awoke, she was gone, and Nandina was staring down at me. She nudged the bottle with her foot. You favor drinking alone? I didn't answer. She nodded her disapproval. You realize I'm more married to you than I am to Tates? I'm sorry, I said. What—sorry that's the situation, sorry you had a woman here, or sorry I'm close enough I can smell her on your skin? I needed the money, I said. That's usually a harlot's excuse, she said. She picked up the bottle, threw it as far as she could, and marched back to the cabin.

Mrs. Garth tapped on the door and Milo let her in. She set his lunch tray on the table by the window.

"You ever see a doctor?"

"I see you," Milo said and touched her starched shirt where it puckered over her breast. "You put me right."

"Lately you haven't wanted my company."

"Much on my mind."

"Perhaps I shouldn't have told you."

"Why not? It's no secret Calla moved away from me, and I found comfort with you. It's fair for her to find someone who satisfies her needs."

"Is Miss Martha bringing you down?"

"No, I think Theo is succeeding with her, whereas I would not. Have you another opinion?"

"You know what it is—all of you are too easy with her."

"She's fragile."

"Mr. Theo is making it worse."

"How, exactly?"

"She's in love with him."

"A crush, perhaps. Not uncommon for girls to have them on their teachers."

"I heard her describing to Miss Nadir how she wanted to..."

"To what?"

"It was very specific. Made the two of us carry on like amateurs. I was surprised she knew what she was saying."

"She sneaks in here and probably reads stuff she shouldn't."

Milo sat down at the table and slid the napkin out of its silver ring. "You got a lot of books. How many you read?"

"All of them."

"The one you're writing, what's it about?"

"Some people who lived in Mott County."

"A long time ago?"

"Some people in the county wouldn't think it was," he said. "Know what I mean?"

"The past. People here hold it close."

"Many do."

She watched Milo taste his soup, admiring how he tilted the spoon and raised it to his mouth instead of bending over and slurping. "That book on your desk looks old."

"Ever hear the name *Provender*?"

"Dale Provender. He works for the Forest Service."

"Same family. Civil War, his great-great-grandfather was sheriff. The book belonged to him."

She laughed. "Instead of tomato soup, I should serve you alphabet, lots of broth with lots of little letters in it. Perfect for a writer."

"A strip or two of bacon would be perfect for the grilled cheese you brought me."

"Your missis said not to serve you salty meat. Doctor Tim told her you need to take care better care of your heart."

"He told me to write more love stories."

"You doing that now?"

"In my way I am."

"I'll leave you to it then."

"It's Tuesday."

"You saying you're up for it tonight?"

"Doctor's orders. He told me to exercise more."

An Indian summer afternoon. Theo looked through Jefferson's binoculars at a plateau on the other side of the river. Shrubs and tangles of honeysuckle and blackberry covered the ground. "If your ancestor was a criminal or simply the body of a traveler no one claimed, he might be over there," Jefferson said. "Used to be a cross. I never saw it, but it shows in old photographs. The oak too. A mighty tree. People believed it was alive when the Jamestown was settled."

"Here is where prisoners were hanged?"

"A rope, a sturdy limb, and a horse. A scaffold came later. Bodies were buried close by. The graves were probably already dug. The dead were taken down and put in the earth and that was that. Folks cried or cheered and went home. The graves were never marked. No stones, head or foot. The names of the condemned were entered in the courthouse record, but it was lost when the building burned in 1876. Most likely arson, though an accident from the exuberant celebration of the nation's independence was the official verdict of the committee that investigated the matter."

"What happened to the oak?"

"Souvenir hunters hacked off pieces and disease set in. The county cut down what was left and sold the good parts to a timber company. From time to time a few citizens suggest erecting a fence, but the grief and sorrow of the place—karma you could call it—keep people away. It's spooky how no trees thrive there anymore. They come up, sumac and persimmon mostly, then they wither as if the land holds no nourishment for them. Same with wildflowers. Jewel weed, Joe-pye, primrose—one week they bloom, next week they die."

Theo handed Jefferson his binoculars and they walked back to the Blazer. Half an hour later they were seated near the Wurlitzer, listening to "Gentle on my Mind," which was barely old enough for Ralph to include it in the Wurlitzer's selections. Jefferson preferred to hear John Hartford sing, not Glen Campbell. After all, Hartford wrote the song. "Not fond of the banjo," Ralph said, adding that Dolley's door was always open, or mostly was, and Jefferson was free to walk any time it suited him.

Connie brought drinks and menus. The previous night a student from the college had celebrated turning twenty-one—Peter Dillingham. Boasted how he planned to break into the Castle. There was a damsel in distress who required saving. Bought a round for the house.

"A few drinks and folks say lots of crazy things," Connie said.

She took the food orders. Glen Campbell sang "Galveston" and "By the Time I get to Phoenix," songs he didn't write, Jefferson was quick to point out. Otherwise, he kept to himself. Fine with Theo, who enjoyed listening to the music and remembering autumn evenings when his uncle played the piano. Melancholy songs about love that never turned out right.

A mile-long gravel lane bordered by sycamores led from the highway to the Castle. On the ride home Jefferson stopped at the curve halfway. He wanted to talk about Calla. Behind her disdain there was disappointment, behind her isolation and indifference were longing and desire going to waste.

"She kissed me once," he said. "Then she apologized. She wasn't used to wine at lunch. Milo had finished several glasses and snoozed on the sofa. She had scarcely touched her first glass. It won't happen again, she said. I heard that as a warning to herself, not an apology to me. Ever since she's treated me like I'm an unwanted guest. How does she treat you?"

Theo took his time answering. "We're friends," he said.

"You were always wanted. I wasn't because I wasn't a way out."

"What are you getting at?"

"The door was opened before. There was a month when the library committee played three-handed bridge. You've opened the door wider. When the time is right, Calla will walk through it and make her way without you. Belva will be waiting."

The hills turned brown. The sky turned gray. Tates killed a hog and bled it. I helped him scald it and hoist it on a gambrel stick so we could scrape and gut the animal, then leave it overnight.

He ran his hand over Nandina's belly and told her not to wait up. The next day was her birthday, and he would return from town with a present. She protested she did not need one, but his mind was made up. Off he went.

She took my hand and we walked awhile. She inquired if my mind was made up about leaving. I remembered her saying I was more her husband than Tates had ever been and answered I had not decided.

We lingered under a beech tree, caressing and kissing until the dark surrounded us. Because of the child, she would not lie with me, but I understood where she felt pleasure and touched her there until she clutched me, shivered, and cried out my name. I finally felt at home with it.

For dinner she served chicken she had roasted, potatoes, and beans. I remarked that Tates could not find a meal as satisfying in town. She replied that the nourishment he craved flowed from a bottle and his companions were men up to no good and women who gave into their needs, though she felt sorrow for them who made a life of such work.

She wanted to know about my life, how it would be if I had returned to where I started from. What did I miss? Had I promised myself to anyone? I had not, I said and told how my parents had passed. I lived in a cabin to myself on property deeded me from my father, separate from what he gave to my brother, who was married and had children and occupied the house where we were born. I suppose I would be seated before a fire, reading a book by candlelight. The Bible? she asked. I admitted I was a poor follower of Christian habits. Did not all soldiers carry Bibles with them? Most, I said. She wished we had a book now so I might read the words aloud to her.

If her child was a girl, she would name her Sarah Bethlehem Croft and call her Sarah Beth. Yet she was sure she carried a boy—William Bethlehem

Croft. William. Did I approve? Of course, I said. I almost told her that my brother was named William, called Willie, which he little cared for. However, I thought it best not to increase the sparse biography I had already created for myself, some of it true, some of it not.

The notion of leaving nagged me. Finally, I nestled into the hay and slept.

MARTHA SAT ON THE window seat, Miss Nadir, as ever, close by. Martha saw beams of light, then Jefferson's Blazer came into view. The car stopped where she could look down. A woman sitting in the back seat changed places with Theo, who got out of the front seat, setting off a security light. Jefferson drove away. Theo unlocked the service door where the delivery man from the market carried in the groceries Calla or Mrs. Garth ordered over the phone.

Miss Nadir said, I know what you're thinking. You shouldn't do it. Why not? Martha asked. Haven't you flirted enough with the man? Miss Nadir answered. Stay here if you want, Martha said.

A few minutes later Martha, barefoot, crept up the stairs and along the hall toward Theo's room. His door was open. She could see a bed and a table with a lamp beside it. A toilet flushed, then Theo appeared. She stepped back and pressed against the dingy wallpaper that pictured a repeating hunting scene—riders, fields, forests, hounds, and a russet fox.

The floor squeaked as Theo moved about. She leaned forward again, watching him, his back turned to her. Naked, he disappeared, then reappeared in profile, lean and tall. Had he glanced sideway he would have caught her stunned in the doorway, staring at every shape and shadow of his body until a robe concealed it. She gasped and silently retreated down the hall toward the stairs. She crouched and looked back. Theo was walking in the opposite direction where another flight of stairs led to Calla's room. Cautiously, Martha followed. When she saw Calla reach across the bed and raise the sheet and Theo's robe wrinkle around his ankles, the floor tilted, she gulped for breath. Trembling, she slunk away, head spinning, eyes stinging with tears.

AHEAD, BELVA SAW A shape hunched along the roadside. A vagrant, she thought, or a local who had drunk too much, or one of the lost souls who lived in the shanties and tents out of sight in the slopes of rhododendrons above the river. People who survived on what they could buy with the money they earned selling cans and bottles they salvaged and rabbits and squirrels they trapped near forgotten creeks where old-timers had carried out baptisms or stilled whiskey, depending on the need or the season.

Belva slowed. The shape was shrouded in fur. Belva stopped. The shape turned around. A face squinted into the lights. Belva switched them off. Enough moon for her to appraise the coat, the kind she had only seen spoiled women in movies wear.

"I'm Belva," she said. "Who are you?"

"Martha," a small voice answered.

"Where are you going?"

"Don't know."

"I'm going home. You're coming with me."

Belva's trailer was a double-wide set on a patch of pavers at the edge of a landing above the river. The owner rented canoes and kayaks to day-trippers who cooked on grills and ate at one of the half-dozen picnic tables and watched the river rushing over rocks where often a heron stood patiently to snatch its supper from the curling water.

Martha followed Belva up the steps and waited, as if spellbound, for instructions. "First, take off your coat and tell me why you were walking along the highway at two in the morning."

"I'm running away."

"From home?"

"Yes, ma'am."

"Skip the *ma'am*. I'm Belva. Belva Morris. You are Martha what?"

"Drew."

"Like Drew Castle Drews?"

"Yes…Belva."

"You're running away from the Castle?"

"Yes."

"And you don't know where you're running to?"

"No…I…mean, yes."

"You're not…" Belva sat down and studied Martha. She was dressed in her favorite leggings, a sweatshirt with the outline of the Tower Bridge sent from London, and thick-soled walking shoes Jefferson had given her at Christmas. She had finally worn them. "Are you the daughter who never goes outside?"

"You know me?"

"You're certainly talked about."

"Miss Nadir said I was."

"And she is?"

"A friend. She didn't want to come with me."

"Is this your maiden voyage?"

"I'm still shaking."

"I see that."

Martha followed Belva to the kitchen space. "You're how old?"

"Seventeen."

"Old enough," Belva said and tipped whiskey into two glasses.

Martha tasted and coughed. "Burns."

"Meant to." Belva pointed to a chair. "Sit." Martha did and swallowed more whiskey. "So—the sky didn't fall on you, the earth didn't split open and swallow you up. You survived."

"So far. I didn't know there were so many stars."

"What happened?"

"You stopped for me. Like the Dickinson poem—because I could not stop for death, death stopped for me."

"Not sure I understand the connection. I meant why did you decide to introduce yourself to the world tonight?"

"May I tell you tomorrow?"

"It *is* tomorrow."

"Can I stay here? Not forever, of course."

"Of course."

"May I have more whiskey?"

"Take mine." Belva pushed her glass across the table. "Your parents are going to miss you. I'd better talk to them before they call the sheriff."

"They won't notice I'm gone, not for a while. I'm not an early riser."

"Theo Vos is your tutor?"

"Let's forget about him."

"Are you recovered enough to sleep?"

"I would like to lie down."

The couch made into a bed. Belva showed Martha the bathroom and gave her a toothbrush and offered a pair of cotton pajamas, but Martha preferred to sleep in her shirt and leggings that felt familiar. "If you want to, you can leave a light on," Belva said.

Martha remembered pulling the coat off the hanger in the closet, the mink her mother had inherited from her mother and never wore because there was no place to wear it to. Martha remembered Duncan rousing himself from the cushion of blankets where he slept in the corner of the kitchen and following her to the service door. She opened it and told him to stay. She stepped outside and gasped. The sky was wider and deeper than she imagined, the stars more than she could have imagined, their patterns, so compact in pictures, flung widely into space.

She shivered and swallowed. No more the familiar, reassuring scents of clothes and cooking, woodsmoke, even the microscopic decaying of paper, fabrics, and skin. Only the rush of cold and flinty air rasping her throat, stinging her eyes.

The skeletal trees welcomed her into the darkness. At first, she took tiny steps to keep from falling—the ground, the visual evidence of her elemental mother, was harder and denser than she expected. To fall and injure herself would be the punishment she deserved for leaving her sanctuary and entering the realm of air where people went about living lives predestined to grief. The Castle's architect understood that thick walls were a metaphor in physical form of the necessity to avoid the disorder of the world as much as possible. The realm of earth was simple and pure. People went about it, walked its surface, but only those who acknowledged it as their mother abided in its peace and security. The children of air and fire and water brought anguish and devastation. They wavered in their priorities. They loved one story, then cast it aside and loved another. They loved a person, then cast the person aside and loved another. They made promises. They did not keep them.

Martha remembered the wings of clouds, a frigid moon, then the flare of lights behind her. Where are you going? the woman asked and Martha had answered to herself, What does it matter?

Martha reached over and turned off the light.

"UP EARLY TODAY, MR. Milo. Way ahead of the missus." Mrs. Garth set a plate of buttered toast beside his coffee cup. The same breakfast every morning, about as much as his stomach tolerated.

"I am," he said.

"Something got you worried?"

"No more than usual."

"It's my opinion that men your age worry more than women."

"And how many men of my age have you known?"

"Known in the broadest sense, or something more specific?"

"Known *well* but not necessarily *intimately*."

"More than a dozen. They were all worriers. Mostly about their bodies, how they were wearing out, what did this pain mean or that one, and how would they die."

"You don't ponder death?"

"Not yet. Too much else on my mind."

"Such as?"

"Keeping you and the missus fed and the house in order. You may have noticed the plumbing is making noises."

"It always complains close to winter."

"Louder every year."

"What else?"

"Miss Martha—mostly her urges. Then there's her screwball philosophy."

"What about her urges?"

"That boy from the college got her started, touching her, making suggestions, stirring her up. Now she flirts with Mr. Theo. No telling what more she would like to do."

"How does he respond?"

The answer was simple enough. Mrs. Garth did the laundry. Calla had company. Martha didn't. "He is teacherly."

"What should we do about Martha?"

"Convince her if she steps outside, all the catastrophes she imagines won't happen."

"That's the screwball philosophy department. I'll let her work it out."

The phone rang. Milo went into the hall to answer it. When he returned, Mrs. Garth was pouring Calla's coffee. "Earth and sky are doing like they always do," he said.

"Milo, what are you talking about?"

"Our daughter isn't here."

"Hallelujah," Mrs. Garth shouted, then apologized. "Oh, Lord, not that Dillingham boy, is it?"

"No boy. A woman named Belva called. She found Martha wandering along the highway. Martha's at her place right now."

Calla said, "She's not hurt or anything?"

"She's fine,' Milo said.

"Leaving here was her idea, no one forced her?"

"Apparently."

"Now what?"

"Let's find out what other ideas she has."

"Meaning?

"Let her decide what she wants to do. You know this Belva? She said she was a friend of Theo's."

"I saw them together at the Laurel. Wilfred told me his opinion. It was favorable."

"Let's hope he's right. Theo up yet?"

"He's slow lately," Mrs. Garth said. "Want me to wake him?"

"Let me," Calla said and left the room.

"Eunice, why are you smiling?"

"Just imagining all the adventures Miss Martha is going to have."

Milo suspected it was more than that. "What else are you imagining?"

"She might go to school and not need a tutor anymore."

"Theo's not to your liking?"

"Miss Martha gives more attention to him than what he's trying to teach her. It's not healthy."

"Didn't you ever have special thoughts about any of your teachers?"

"Mine were women, mean as snakes, all of them."

Calla reappeared. "Theo will be right down," she said. "I told him what happened. He knows where Belva lives. He'll bring Martha back."

Milo carried his cup and saucer to the sink. "You don't need me."

SEVERAL TIMES DURING THE night Milo awakened and thought about the word *buggy* that Provender had written in his notes and underlined. Milo found where he had left off.

> Tates' voice woke me. He was talking sober and softly to Button, the horse he was leading into the barn. In the morning I saw the buggy outside the barn. Instead of her usual smile, Nandina only nodded and set a plate of grits and eggs before me. I wasn't used to seeing Tates so early. He had finished his breakfast. In town he had met up with Kitts, who had doctored Nandina when she had needed it. Because she had lost one child, he advised Tates to bring her to visit him so he could counsel her how best she might avoid losing another. He had even lent Button and a buggy.
>
> Nandina stared at the ground. Tates hitched Button to the buggy. I helped her climb up. I watched

until she was out of sight. Wasn't long before Vesper came into view. That's Mr. Davis's horse, she said. One of only two of his that tolerated traces. I told her what Tates had told us, the visit to town to see the doctor. I been to see him, she said. She raised her jacket and patted her flat belly. One of Davis's other horses had bucked and thrown her.

I said I was sorry about her condition. She did not want a child, she said. Mr. Davis wanted one. She stared at me and shook her head as if I lacked understanding. Nandina? I uttered. What didn't I know?

A trip to town, perhaps, but not to see the doctor. Tates had gambled away his land to Davis, who let him keep it in exchange for Nandina, who would remain Davis's property until her child was born. Davis's wife died and he had lost his two sons in the war. A girl child would be Nandina's and she could return to living with Tates. A boy child would be Davis's, and after she had nursed it, she could, if she wished, go back to Tates, if he would have her.

You were sweet to me, Vesper said. She touched my cheek. She knew Mr. Davis had advised me to leave the county. Now was a good time, she said.

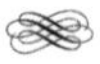

BELVA TOLD THEO THAT while she was showering Martha had phoned Dillingham. She had kept the information he had given her before Calla dismissed him. Belva was half-dressed when she heard Martha slip out. "I might run nearly naked after you but not her," Belva said. He could tell Mrs. Drew that her coat was safe. Martha had left it and taken one of Belva's jackets.

"She won't go far," Theo said.

"What do you want to bet? Dillingham has a car and a credit card."

"I bet he lacks patience."

"You appear to have too much of it. Shouldn't we get after her?"

"He'll want to please her eyes, excite her with the world. Mott County isn't going to do it."

"Holcombe County will?"

"It's got Almsville. I doubt he'll drive her to Atlanta or Charleston or even Charlotte."

"She'll need clothes. Travel magazines call Almsville the showplace of the mountains. Fancy shops. Fancy restaurants and hotels. What are we waiting for?"

"To give her time to meet the world."

"Time for Dillingham to ply her with gifts before he asks something in return, and we know what that is."

"She might say no."

"He might not listen."

Theo phoned. Calla answered. He said he guessed Dillingham was taking Martha to Almsville. She said she guessed Martha had seen them together. Fleeing the Castle was their punishment.

Belva drove. Her Subaru was more reliable than Theo's Jeep. "I know what you like, and you haven't been spending time with me, so you must be spending time with someone else. From what I hear of your habits from Jefferson and Connie, I think your someone is Miz Calla. She's been fooling us. Beneath those prim plaids and woolens, there's a needy body. Fess up."

"There's more to her than meets the eye," Theo said.

"You could say that about most anyone."

"Could."

"Okay, what's going on with Martha? Why did she flee the Castle?"

"It was time, don't you think?"

"I think there's more to it than that."

THE WORLD BLURRED BY. The radio was distracting. Martha told Peter to turn it off. The monotone of tires and swishing air was music enough. Cars flashed past. Ahead the highway divided into roads spidering in different directions. A cemetery spread down a hillside. Peter said Thomas Wolfe was buried there. "O lost, and by the wind grieved, ghost, come back again." Martha remembered Milo quoting him, but his books were too long for her to finish.

Peter stopped in front of a store. Draped in browns and blacks, the mannequins held out their arms as if saying, Come, let us adorn you.

"I am Mrs. Goff," the woman said. "Welcome to My Lady." She looked at Peter as if asking what Martha required. "Everything," he said. Other women came forward, attendants of a fairy court where Martha would be pampered and worshipped. She was undressed, then dressed in a chatter of suggestions, rejections, and approvals. The attendants bowed and Mrs. Goff led Martha to Peter's admiring gaze. "The sandal strap echoes the mango color of her scarf, which releases the topaz understatement of her blouse. Of course, black silk trousers are classic," Mrs. Goff said. She did not comment on Martha's underwear, whose color, she told Martha, Americans referred to as *nude*, but Europeans called *skin*. "I have fresh skin," she whispered to Peter when they were in the car again.

Buildings towering, gates opening, concrete spiraling, steps, lights, elevator ascending, and there they stood, Peter holding Martha's hand, a hall of mirrors, music softly playing.

"A table near the windows," Peter said. Menus appeared. "And the wine list."

The server scanned Peter's ID but requested none from Martha, who gazed down at the sidewalk and the street. In the blink of an eye, she saw more people than she had seen in her whole life. Bodies in motion whose purposes and destinations she could not imagine, yet there they were as if they traveled back and forth, prisoners in a concrete incarceration who disappeared and reappeared dressed in different clothes, going in the opposite directions.

Glassware gleamed, chandeliers sparkled, waiters bowed. Peter smiled. His eyes—she remembered the book of prints Theo had shown her—yes, Peter's eyes were Parrish blue—and the story Theo told her, how the painter's helper had been Martha's age when she became his lover and stayed with him into his old age. Was Theo hinting at something involving the two of them, he and Martha, she had wondered and hoped it were so. Now, however, she deemed Theo unfaithful, a knight who had forgotten the duty he had sworn to fulfill. Miss Nadir had warned her.

The wine was sweet and fruity, and Theo was far away. Peter opened Martha's hand. His finger traced her lifeline. "Sleepy?" he asked. "Very," she said.

BELVA FOUND A PARKING place on the main square near the Confederate monument. "What's the plan?" she asked.

"We check out hotel garages looking for an older Mercedes with a college parking permit."

"All the hotels?"

"The expensive ones."

The Woodward was closest. They walked through the lobby to the elevators and rode to the parking level. The attendant eyed them but said nothing. They kept walking, up and down the rows of cars, all washed and shiny. No trace of Mott County dust.

The Cheshire was next, less desolate and cold than the Woodward, but a bit shabby. Guests favored dark sedans. The man wore a brown uniform. "Help you folks?"

"My son's not very responsible," Theo said. "There was a party. He went off with someone. I think he left his car here. Mercedes, some age on it."

The man shook his head. "Sure you got the right place? We're not much of a young person's party hotel. Most of our guests are older. Some families been staying here for generations on their trips back and forth to Florida, or locals who remember that writer and his wife bunking here—Fitzgeralds."

"Any advice?" Belva asked.

"Bellevue, the new one with all the marble and glass and stuck-up employees dressed in fancy outfits. The man over there would remember a Mercedes like your son's. He's lucky if they let him leave it. Might tell him to park on the street." The man laughed. "No idea why they named it like they did. Isn't Bellevue a hospital with a bunch of crazy people?"

Two blocks away, sitting in his security booth facing a monitor, the attendant, dressed in a blue uniform, watched Theo and Belva descend the circular stairway from the street to underground parking. He stepped out of the booth and asked for their ticket.

The man's nameplate read Taylor. Belva nudged Theo in the ribs and whispered, "You're on."

"Taylor, my son forgot he had my camera in his car. I think he planned to stop here."

"Make of car?"

"Mercedes, older model. Seen it?"

"And smelled it. I'm no friend of diesels."

"So he *is* here?"

"With a young lady. I heard him praise our dining facilities." Taylor pointed toward a distant wall. "You'll find his vehicle in the last row."

"We'll catch up with him inside," Belva said.

"Lunch is served in the Vance room," Taylor said. The door of the security booth buzzed and closed behind him.

The maître d' was about to hook a velvet rope to the brass pole on the other side of the doorway. "We close at two, sir."

"I believe Peter Dillingham and his friend dined here?"

"He did. He forgot his credit card. I sent it to Reception."

"He booked a room?"

"I certainly hope so. He needed a bit of a rest."

"Wine?"

"Quite so, sir."

Belva slipped her arm through Theo's. "Now what? Reception isn't going to tell you Dillingham's room number."

"Watch," Theo said.

The clerk's nameplate read Ludwig. Theo wrote out a message, folded the paper, and handed it across the desk. "Ludwig, please give this to Mr. Dillingham." Ludwig turned and laid the paper in one of the numbered boxes in the row behind him.

"Third floor, I think, but I couldn't read the room number," Belva said as they walked to the elevators past the wide stairs that led to the ballroom on the mezzanine.

"Good enough," Theo said. The elevator door closed and noiselessly opened on the third floor. Down a hushed corridor they saw a housekeeper's cart. Theo gave Belva twenty dollars and retreated around the corner.

The housekeeper was counting pillowcases. "Excuse me..." She looked up and Belva said, "I need your help," and held out the money.

"*Qué*?" The woman had dark eyes and small hands.

"My daughter…a man brought her here. She is young. He gave her lots to drink. Alcohol. Understand?"

The woman nodded. "*Sí.*"

"I want to find her…before…you know…" Belva reached out. "Please."

The woman tucked the money into the pocket of her smock and lifted a clipboard from her cart. "*Trescientos veinticinco,* three twenty-five," she said. She pointed to her watch. "They just here. An hour, maybe."

"*Gracias,*" Belva said and went to find Theo.

I asked Vesper where Davis would keep Nandina and would not Tates understand the gravity and error of such negotiation that deprived her of choice or escape from his vices and their consequences? Would he not beg for release and promise payment even if that were all his property and by such arrangement, he and Nandina would need leave the land and seek employment and shelter wherever they might find it?

Your foolishness goes forth as innocence, and your innocence as ignorance, Vesper replied. She took my hand and kissed my cheek. Hurd's Inn, she said, was where Davis would keep Nandina. The name was unfamiliar to me. What Vesper knew of it the inn was on a rise above the river close to Almsville. Before the war people came there to escape the heat of the Lowcountry. Now, newly reopened, the inn welcomed clergy and others of means and respectability, who did not find the lodgings favored by drovers and those of questionable identity to their liking. Vesper assured me that Nandina would be well cared for. Hurd himself professed medical knowledge. Once when he visited Davis, he had called her into the house so Hurd might examine her. She had stood before him while he peered through a special glass at every inch of her body and probed it with a dry finger. He called her lassie and used words she was unfamiliar with.

I asked if Vesper could steer a boat. She understood that I intended to rescue Nandina. If I were a cat, Vesper said, I would be running out of lives. I asked if she referred to the war. That and skinning with another man's wife and claiming to be someone who you are not, she said.

What does skinning mean? I inquired. What you and I have done, rubbing our skin parts together, or don't you remember? I do, most vividly, I said. There was pleasure in it then? she asked. Indeed, I said. And what is it I often see you take from your pocket? she asked. I showed her my buckeye, telling her it was a nut and not much good for anything except if you buffed it, you could make it shine. A shiny one brought you good luck. If I knew where they grow, she said, I'd know where you came from.

A Do-Not-Disturb placard hung on the door. Belva knocked and called out "Housekeeping." She knocked again. The door opened. Martha pressed her finger to her lips. "He's sleeping," she said.

"You all right?" Theo asked.

"Disappointed."

They walked toward the elevators. The housekeeper peeped around the corner and smiled.

"Nice clothes," Theo said.

"I didn't take them off."

"I didn't ask."

"You wanted to."

"What happened?" Belva said.

"At lunch Peter drank most of a bottle of wine. He paid for a room. I used the toilet. When I came out, he was sprawled on the bed, asleep."

In the elevator Martha held Belva's hand and leaned her head against Belva's shoulder. The elevator whooshed and settled. Silent doors slid open.

When Martha heard the music, she stopped and stared across the lobby at the woman in a shimmering dress seated near the fountain playing a harp. Enchanted, Martha listened, the notes drawing her closer and closer. They died away. The woman lifted her hands from the strings. "Can you teach me?" Martha asked.

THE EVENING SETTLED IN. "Theo, you left her?" Calla said.

"Not exactly. I know where the woman—"

"A name, please."

"McKenzie."

"Mrs.?"

"Miss. She has an apartment near the hotel."

"I don't care if she has a penthouse. Milo, say something."

"Ah, the harp, as Coleridge so wistfully observed, 'the long sequacious notes Over delicious surges sink and rise Such a soft floating witchery of sound As twilight Elfins make, when they at eve Voyage on gentle gales from Fairy-land.'" Milo refilled his glass. "We used to have some recordings of Celtic harps. Not sure where they've got to."

Calla reached for Milo's glass, drank some of his whiskey, and took a deep breath. "I'm calm." Another drink and she handed the glass to Milo. "Okay, you found Martha at the Bellevue in a room with Peter Dillingham. He bought her clothes, fed her lunch, planned to have sex, drank too much, and passed out. No protests, no arguments, Martha is on her way home until she hears a woman playing a harp—"

"The 'soft floating witchery,'" Milo interrupted.

"Okay, she's bewitched, asks the woman to teach her to play the instrument, and Theo says fine, no problem."

"There was a problem," Theo said. "Martha wasn't going to go with us."

"What exactly did she say?"

"I'm staying."

"Oh," Milo said.

"Oh, what, Milo?"

"I wish she had expressed herself more dramatically. After all, the decision deserved it."

"Milo..." Calla shook her head. "Theo, what arrangements did you make?"

"If Martha would help McKenzie with tasks like cooking and shopping, she would teach her to play. She has a smaller harp in the apartment. We would be welcome to visit any time, either at the apartment or the hotel."

"Milo, your opinion?"

"*Sequacious* is a lovely word. We should use it more."

In the dining room Mrs. Garth served Calla and Milo roast beef, green beans, and mashed potatoes. In the kitchen she fixed Theo a plate of hash and eggs. She sat and drank a mug of tea while he ate.

"Going to try your luck tonight? Or do you think the boss lady's precious portal is closed to you now?"

"I think I'll wait for an invitation."

"She may invite you to pack your bags, but I'd bet against it."

"How did Martha find out?"

"About you and the missus—not much happens here that Martha doesn't discover. Like Milo says, Miss Martha lurks, silent as the soul, or some such nonsense."

"And you?"

"I do the laundry and the cleaning. I'm aware of conjugal activity."

"Martha left because of me and Calla?"

"It's you that put a smile on the missus's face."

"She's not smiling now."

"Mr. Theo, smart as you are, you should understand what's happening."

"Tell me."

"You showed up and changed how things work here. Relationships, I mean. You've become more Miss Martha's father than Milo is, and Calla's lover more than Milo has been for some while now. You're like a husband, only better."

"Sort of leaves Milo out of things."

"Come now, Mr. Theo. It's no mystery. I'm Mr. Milo's lover, as much a one as he has use for. This part of the state is used to earthquakes—minor ones, nothing major. Martha's leaving shakes the ground a bit, but the structure holds. You and the missus, you should go to the city. Check on Martha. Confirm to yourselves she's all right and learning what she wants to learn."

"Anything else?"

"All those hotels. Get a room. Go at it like rabbits."

VI

"You have a boat?" Vesper asked.

"Don't even have fit clothes for warmth and travel," I answered.

She cozied up to me and rubbed against my body. "Is skinning only thing you're good at?" she asked.

I don't know why I answered like I did. Maybe I was thinking ahead of myself to what might befall us at Hurd's Inn. I said I was an able marksman.

"But you got no gun," she said. I told her I might know where there was one. She squinted one eye and said, "Maybe an Enfield rifle?"

I stood there open mouthed. She joked I looked as comfortable and content as a hog waltzing on ice. She turned serious then.

"You shot that man Grundy or whatever, the one who was lying in the casket in the window, didn't you?"

I answered that Tates had spoken of it, but I had no knowledge of the deceased or his circumstances. She replied if she didn't care for me as much as she did, she would speak of me to Sheriff Provender. Might be some reward money, hard currency you could test with your dog tooth, not those scraps of paper the government in Washington claimed were worth the numbers printed on them.

No matter what I planned, I needed better clothes and boots. Vesper had money that Davis had given her, or she had helped herself to. I had what Davis had given me. We rode the horse she had borrowed from Davis's stable to town and left the animal at the livery stable so Davis could eventually claim it. We went to Duff's where Tates had bought me clothes before. We told him we needed respectable travelling attire. For me and my daughter, I said, which is how Vesper and I decided to present ourselves. I came away with a wool suit and vest. Vesper acquired a black bonnet and mourning dress that Duff's wife lent to widows who lacked proper attire to attend a service and burial. By evening we had shopped for stockings and footwear and, clothed in respectability, we found lodging at the Laurel, which, owing to difficult times, had recently opened for guests. After a supper better than I had eaten in a long time, I was offered a sherry in a parlor where a fire blazed and a woman Vesper's age played a spinet and sang several songs. I closed my eyes and listened. "'Oh, the years creep slowly by, Lorena, The snow is on the grass again. The sun's low down the sky, Lorena, The frost gleams where the flow'rs have been.'" How many times around a dwindling campfire I had heard the words and wished I were home and not a soldier.

Vesper and I had separate rooms, but she slept in mine. Did I have a sweetheart where I came from?

she asked. I answered that I did not. She explored me and I held her hand to quiet it. Is Nandina why you won't love me now? she asked. I answered I would not because where I was going, she could not follow. I wanted my words to sound ominous and portentous, but they even sounded hollow to me. Horseshit, she said and laughed and commented that a bit of skinning would help us both to sleep, and why, otherwise, was she in my bed? Much about her body and argument were persuasive. Later I realized the mistake I had made.

THE RADIATOR CLANKED. CALLA pulled the covers up to her chin. "I hope this wasn't a mistake," she said.

"Tonight, or all the others?" Theo asked.

She searched for his hand. "I feel Martha is watching us. The more she's gone, the more she's here." Calla pressed Theo's palm against skin where she was still wet. "Thing is, I feel guilty she's gone, but emotionally I don't miss her as much as Milo does. I told him to do what you told me to—phone the McKenzie woman and ask to speak with Martha. By the way, I forgot to tell you Martha wants to be called Lily now, after Lily Neill. Apparently, she's a famous harpist. I asked if Miss Nadir would approve. Martha—Lily—said she and Miss Nadir aren't communicating with each other anymore."

"Would you prefer I leave so you and Milo can settle into a new routine?"

"Strange, but his routines always center around loss."

"What if you left him?"

"I'm not ready to forsake Milo, nor he to leave me, but sometimes I imagine you and I together, somewhere warm, a Caribbean island,

Saint Something. A few months of sea and sun and pleasure before regrets and recriminations set in and I wrinkle like old leather and people think I pay you for your services and we become a cliché."

Theo lifted Calla's hand and kissed her fingertips. "Let's stay home," he said.

Calla snuggled against his side. "Theo, where is your home? You never talk about where you grew up or your family."

"Does it matter?"

"Sweet Theo, even if home isn't the physical place we return to, we go there in our minds. Little by little, memories take over. Tell me about your parents."

"Both were teachers—history and social studies. My father—"

"Name?"

"Peter Vos. Besides teaching he raised tulips."

"Very Dutch. You said Katherine was your mother's name."

"Katherine Stroud."

"Sounds German."

"She was more French. She was always humming 'La Vie en Rose.'"

"Grandparents?"

"Farmers on both sides. So were their parents and generations before them. Lots of farmers and every now and then a teacher. Some of the Stroud land is an airport now. Private planes and charters. We could fly to Saint Whatever."

"We agreed to stay home."

Wind rattled the windows. Calla sighed and drifted into sleep. Theo closed his eyes. Twice a year his mother tended the private cemetery separated from the runway by an iron fence, pruning, mowing, and raking. He remembered her staring at the stone: PLYMOUTH STROUD, 1839–? SOLDIER AND PATRIOT. SON OF THE EARTH. SERVANT OF THE LORD.

In the morning Theo was surprised to find Mrs. Garth pouring Jefferson a cup of coffee.

"Milo wants to see me early," he said.

Mrs. Garth looked at her watch, then focused on Theo. "Nine o'clock is not early. Not for folks with chores to do."

"Early for Milo, isn't it?"

"Not since Miss Martha went. I saw him near eight walking Duncan in the orchard. Poor old animal can hardly keep up." She warmed a muffin for Theo. "When I'm old and put out to pasture, I hope some kind soul offers me a good slug of rye instead of marching me around in the cold." She chuckled to herself and set about polishing the silver Calla had said needed doing. Jefferson and Theo excused themselves to find Milo.

"Jefferson, since your gallery is closed until the leaky roof is fixed, and Theo, since Miss Martha has traded you for a stringed instrument, I believe you both have time on your hands to assist me."

"Guess so," Jefferson said and sat down beside Theo on the couch.

Milo continued, "The Laurel was a private home until the Stocks started taking in guests to make ends meet—autumn 1865. The second of November Provender scribbled some cryptic notes and questions about a visit from Duff, who made caskets, buried people, and kept their clothes to sell. He told Provender he sold a suit to a man who stepped into another room, took off what he wore, and put on the suit. The man said the woman with him was his daughter, but the more Duff studied her the more he suspected otherwise. She resembled a young woman people had pointed out to him as leading a profligate life. Lots of folks were pretending to be families while scheming to trick folks into giving them money, what there was of it."

"Nothing unusual about buying clothes even if they came off a dead person. What's got you interested?" Jefferson asked.

"The man came in wearing trousers that a farmer had bought from Duff months before. At the time he told Duff a soldier was helping with the farm and his clothes were near worn out."

Jefferson shrugged and glanced at Theo. "What am I missing?"

Theo turned to Milo. "A connection? Who to whom? What to what?"

Milo said, "I think Provender was asking himself the same questions."

"How are we supposed to help?"

"Jefferson, you and Theo are on good terms with Wilfred Stock. He and I have a perpetual disagreement about a bill I never paid. Our friendship is strained, to say the least. His records of the Laurel go back to the beginning. I know because the town library once tried to acquire them for its archive, but he wouldn't give them or sell them, either one. He won't show them to me, but he might to the both of you. Provender's note suggests you're searching out names of guests who could have stayed at the Laurel the November in question. A man and a woman. She might be his daughter or might not. Treat yourself to lunch. The cook over there serves a fine rabbit stew. Somewhere in his book Mr. Wells remarked on how exceedingly tasty Mott County rabbits were. They still are."

What mistake are you cursing over? Vesper asked. I answered I wouldn't say until she told me what she knew about Enfield rifles and where I might find one. She replied plain enough. She said caps, powder, shot and an Enfield were waiting in a crevice of rock up the slope close to where the body of the man named Grundy was found.

How do you know? I asked, though from the accuracy of what she already said, I feared what she would say. Estes Grundy was the man's name. She had encountered him panning for gold, trying to find a trace of it that might encourage him to keep prospecting for more. She was wanting money, and he was wanting company.

He had stripped down to his drawers. She was reclining on a blanket. His horse was tethered up the hill. She was studying him, wondering why he wasn't paying attention to her because she wasn't wearing much more than he was. He must have heard something. He crouched down and observed the river and whispered there was a man washing himself. Then he swore and reached for his trousers. There was a scabbard with a bayonet on his belt. While he snaked toward the shore, she grabbed up the trousers that Preacher Landry had given her. According to him, her chest wasn't womanly, and her slender body was like a man's, so a man's clothes suited her. She said she never did like corsets and skirts wide enough to hide a sow and piglets under.

You saw everything? I asked. No, she said, not everything. She had scuttled up the hill to the horse. She heard the shot and looked back. She saw me tending to Albert's body. Saw Grundy lying dead and hoped I wouldn't leave him almost naked. She wanted to get his shirt and brogans. They were almost new. Good boots and brogans were almost impossible to find. She would have waited longer, but the horse was snorting and neighing. She rode it away, then left it and knew no more of

Grundy until weeks later Davis told her where a body had been discovered. The dead man wore a Union soldier's pants. Belt and buckle were Union too, so was the haversack Sheriff Provender located nearby. He searched around and found a shirt and a jacket. Laid in the blanket where she and Grundy had lain, the dead man was carried to a skiff and transported to Elland. She guessed one of the men helping Provender had found the brogans and didn't tell about it.

This time Duff not only offered to embalm the body but also to display it in his window to advertise his skills and entice people to believe the extra expense of preserving a loved one's remains and make it lovely awhile longer so distant kin could travel to see the deceased one last time was worth the cost. When Provender stopped by, Duff told him that the jacket he found didn't belong to the same man.

Vesper brushed her hair away from her eyes. She said that the sheriff supposed three men had been at the river. I said she could have told Provender what she knew.

I knew where there was a rifle, she said. Didn't know it was an Enfield until she went looking for it. She had heard soldiers praise them for being good guns. She considered she could sell it, but she worried Provender would catch up with her and be wanting her to tell him what she had told me. Worse, he might accuse her of participating in the deaths of two people even if all she did was not telling all that she had seen.

Vesper smiled her freckly smile. Besides, she said, Davis figured I wasn't a Confederate making his way home even though I talked like I was. He never said anything to Tates or Provender because he guessed I was more useful alive than dead. So far it hasn't worked out that way, I replied. For sure won't, she said, if I spoiled Davis' plan for Nandina.

"NO, SIR, NO RABBIT on the menu." Mason pointed to the windows. "Plenty outside. You snare one, the cook will serve you up a fine meal, and I for sure can pour you an excellent vintage to go with it."

Jefferson and Theo took Mason's recommendation and ordered trout and almondine potatoes. The wine was compliments of Wilfred, who missed having Theo and Miss Belva for guests. She had stayed a couple of nights, but her company wasn't as couth as Theo.

After lunch and some discussion of privacy and the delicate condition of an historical document, Jefferson and Theo were welcome to examine the only record Wilfred could or would provide, a leather-bound volume of foxed pages in which Chatham Stock, Wilfred's great-grandfather, wrote down the names of guests, or the names they chose to go by, and what they owed. Guests weren't required to sign their own names or give their addresses. Chatham had saved more than one man from the embarrassment of not being able to write anything at all.

"A few identities are obviously false." Wilfred pointed to the entry 26TH OCTOBER, ARTHUR KING, SUPPER AND LODGING, 11$. "Chatham was liberal minded. He couldn't afford not to be. If a guest said the woman with him was his wife, that's what Chatham recorded.

Otherwise, he entered so-and-so and companion. Later, if he knew her name, he might add it after the guests had left."

"Like this one? '1ST NOVEMBER. P. PUTNAM AND MISS PUTNAM, PARENTHESIS VESPER L,'" Jefferson said.

"Right. You can see *Vesper* and *L* are a different ink. Chatham wrote it later. Whoever she was, Miss Putnam was not P. Putnam's daughter."

"Vesper Landry," Jefferson said. "Chatham would have called her Landry because he took care of her, but they weren't kin. It probably amused Chatham to think of her that way."

"Jefferson, I forget you carry a lot of our history in that handsome head of yours."

"I don't know that much about her, except she could read and write, sail a skiff, and was intelligent and attractive."

"Did she use that for professional advantage?"

"I doubt she held back when something might be gained."

"Might have gained a pound or two. Supper and libations cost six dollars. Must have eaten well."

Jefferson turned the pages, then handed the book to Wilfred. "Have you ever read Wells' book on the Western counties? He mentions Chatham."

"The business with the bodies. Chatham inviting folks to drink to celebrate fewer Yankees being alive to gloat over the South suffering defeat. They forget that Chatham took charge of the body pulled from the river and gave the man a Christian burial on his own property, not on that forsaken place where they hanged people. Paid to have the man unburied too."

"What property?"

"Where the feed store is."

"Did Chatham keep a record of his expenses?"

"I've got it somewhere. Take a while to find."

"Let me know when you do," Jefferson said.

VII

Milo settled into his chair, Provender's book on his lap. Fuss at Hurd's, Provender wrote. He started late, stayed over. STABLE FEE, SUPPER, BED 9$. Milo smiled to himself and began to type.

I could have lain in bed with Vesper a long time, but our room was over the kitchen. Early I heard voices and the rattle of activity. We ate and I paid our bill. In one of the Stock's privies, we changed into our old clothes, cramming our new ones into Vesper's carpetbag. She stood back as I arranged with a drover to carry us in his wagon as far as Hurd's. The drover studied us, trying to make out if Vesper, wearing boots, trousers, a long jacket, her hair bunched under her hat, was a man or a woman. Man, he guessed. Otherwise, he might have forgone a bit of money for a bit of pleasure.

The woman with him didn't seem to care one way or the other. She was weathered and stern and clenched a pipe in her crooked teeth. If you approached too close, she spat at your feet. The drover and another man walked ahead, tending the cattle. Mid-afternoon we reached the inn. A man dressed like a servant rushed out and told the drover to keep moving. Hurd's was no place for beasts of the field and people involved in herding or animal trade. While the man was insulting the drover, Vesper and I climbed down from the wagon. We inquired about work. Vesper took off her hat. My daughter, I said. The man's name was Bose. Some chores in the kitchen, washing up, he told her. Nothing for me unless I could shoe a horse. I asked how much to sleep in the stable. Fifty cent, he said. Vesper opened the bag and showed him her dress. He agreed it made her presentable enough to collect dishes from the tables.

Vesper followed Bose to the inn. After the stable man promised me a clean stall, I wandered down to the river. Ptolemy Green owned three skiffs. Either he or Abel, his helper, made regular trips back and forth to Almsville, sailing if the wind was right, rowing if need be, which cost extra because of hiring another man. Ptolemy named a price and took half of it to reserve a boat. He was willing to set off before dawn and didn't need to know the reason. He required three dollars more, though.

Vesper learned that Nandina took her evening meal in her room. Davis had spread the story she was widowed and frail and suffered deep melancholy since the death of her husband. She read, took solitary walks, and seldom spoke with anyone except Hurd or Davis, who dined together in the public room and lingered over Port that Hurd had hidden in the rafters to save from looters during the war.

Luck was with us. Bose sent Vesper and another woman to gather Nandina's dishes and tidy her chamber for the evening. Recognizing Vesper, Nandina sent the other woman downstairs to fetch some Port for herself. Vesper told Nandina I had hired a boat. On her walks she had seen Ptolemy's enterprise and would be at the river before dawn. She did not show Vesper the pistol Davis had loaded for her and told her to keep close. Next morning, she appeared hastening toward the river in the lingering dark. Bose's snarling dog almost upon her, she withdrew the pistol from her reticule, the only property she carried, and shot the animal. Stunned, we watched the dog fall and die. Minutes later, the wind in the sail, Bose cursed us from the shore. I made out some of what he said. Nandina had made off with money. Ptolemy pretended not to hear. The skiff sailed on, but I feared our luck had turned around.

THE SITUATION WAS UNUSUAL, late afternoon someone pounding on his door. Milo opened it. "Martha's gone," Calla said. "I drove to McKenzie's apartment to visit with her. No one was there. The manager said McKenzie quit her job at the hotel and took off with Martha. McKenzie doesn't like winter. She has plenty of money to do what she wants and do it in style. She's serious about the harp but performing is merely an amusement for her. The manager forwards her mail to Florida." Milo was about to say something. Calla raised her hand. "And…" She pushed Milo backward into his parlor. "And there's more—the manager thinks the young man who called on Martha a couple of times is with them. Guess who." Milo shook his head. "Dillingham."

Milo snickered. "There's a threesome for you."

"Milo, this isn't funny. What are we going to do?"

Milo pointed over Calla's shoulder. Theo stood in the hall. "Ask him."

She spun around. "Theo, you heard?" He nodded.

Milo had poured himself a drink. He leaned in the doorway and watched Calla go up the stairs. He shook his head. "Florida—too much water. I don't care for the sea." He tapped the rim of the glass against his chin. "I'm trying to remember a poem...Yes, 'the sea is but a sound, I would be near it on a sandy mound And hear the steady rushing of the deep, While I lay stinging in the sand with sleep.' Yvor Winters. Read him?" Theo shook his head. "Quite out of fashion now but worth a try."

"Milo, do you object to my going after Martha with Calla?"

"Dear boy, I would object if you did not, but I wonder if the errand is in Martha's best interest."

"She's seventeen. You can't just let her go off somewhere."

"Her entrance into the world has certainly been unexpected and rather thrilling, really."

"Do you believe she's prepared for the world?"

"I'm relying on the McKenzie woman. I trust harp players." Milo patted Theo's chest. "And I trust you. *Honi soit* and all that. Now, come sit and tell me... how did it go with Wilfred?"

Estelle McKenzie folded the newspaper, looked over the hedge of bougainvillea edging the terrace, picked up her binoculars, and fixed her attention on the beach. Peter had anchored a large yellow umbrella in the sand and was slathering Martha's back with sunscreen. Bringing him was a disappointment. He was as omnipresent as grief. It was impossible to spend time with Martha by herself, or at least sufficient opportunity to get to know her the way Estelle wanted to, which was not with Martha agog each afternoon before a television screen or plugged into one of Peter's music devices, or nights with Peter and Martha tittering in his room. Of course, the more noise they made, the better. In their silences Estelle heard her own heart beating.

She was a lovely woman. When she performed, men undressed her. She knew because they told her so. Women, too, though not as often as she liked. She had invited Martha to watch her dress (do you think this blouse is too sheer for me, this skirt too short for me, perfect for you, though, your long legs, try it on), choose what to wear to the restaurant where she had reserved a table near the fountain. The languid sound of water, she said, reaching out and running her fingers down Martha's tanned arm, so soft, so soothing. Did Peter not think when his eyes were locked with hers that she knew under the table his fingers inched up Martha's thigh?

However much a disappointment and a distraction, Peter was a necessity. Martha was seventeen. People would assume she was a daughter and Peter her boyfriend, a narrative they had agreed on. Estelle had made a pact with herself that Martha, or Lily, as she wished to be called, must remain, in part, a fantasy. Estelle was forty-four. She was already concerned what the legal consequences might be bringing Martha to Florida. Her family was certainly a curious one and no coercion or force was involved, though Estelle chided herself for not writing the Drews to let them know where Martha was and how quickly she had agreed to Estelle's suggestion of a change of scene. Part of the pleasure of Martha's presence was Estelle's fantasy of freeing a lover from the prison of the familiar that surrounded her, satisfying the urges of unexplored passion. As for Estelle's own desires, they must be consummated only in touches and caresses she bestowed on herself.

The thing was, Estelle had not tried to conceal her—their—whereabouts. The tutor—Theo, was it?—was certainly on his way to fetch her home. Doubtful that Martha would refuse to go. The idyll would end. Peter, having phoned his parents to report on a whim he had followed a friend to Florida, would depart as well. Good riddance there.

Estelle set her binoculars aside, raised her face to the sun, and smiled as if posing for a brochure: the satisfied tourist. If performing had taught her anything, it was to hide in plain sight.

Despite the season, the air was mild. The river ran fast and full. Ptolemy pointed to a log house near the shore. He needed refreshment, he said. He eased off the sail rope, letting the current push us while he steered toward a dock that tilted over the water. I saw the worry on Nandina's face. Ptolemy beckoned me to take the tiller. He balanced in the rocking boat and snatched off Vesper's hat. Like I suspected, he said, a lady you are, or a woman at least. From the looks of you, accustomed to male company. He nodded toward the house. You'll find a friendly respite there, a chance to relieve yourself and have a bit of pleasure. Vesper shaded her eyes with her hand. Too early in the day for strong spirits, she said. That is not what I have in mind, Ptolemy replied. What about my friends? she asked. He recommended a stroll to lighten the tedium of travel. I think not, Vesper said. Ptolemy knelt and took back the tiller. Then I think not to our proceeding more, he said.

The sail was slack now. Has been a season, Nandina said, since she had pleasure from a man, and Ptolemy appeared eager and up to it. Perhaps he would care to touch the goods before committing himself. Ptolemy grunted his assent and clambered past Vesper to the bow where Nandina stood, holding onto an oar to steady herself. He commented how he could not judge her figure under the jacket and the skirts she wore but reckoned it was attractive enough to satisfy him. He reached a hand toward her bosom. Nandina seized his arm and pushed him overboard. Amazed, I watched Ptolemy struggling in the current. When he grabbed the gunwale, Nandina raised the oar and struck his hand. He cursed and spit water. The second time she struck his head. Vesper climbed over me and pulled the sail rope taut. Half-dressed, a man came running from the house, Tates by the looks of him, followed by a woman half-dressed herself.

By then we were in the middle of the river again. We could make out Ptolemy thrashing toward the shore. Nandina dropped the oar and crawled past me. She wrapped her arms around Vesper. I could not decide if they were laughing or weeping.

Nandina let go and dried her eyes. Vesper said we would not require Ptolemy's skills to land us. Preacher Landry had owned a boat. He called the French Broad by its Cherokee name—Zillicoah. He referred to it as God's waterway and was fond of gliding upon it, gathering his thoughts about Jesus and creation—the continents, the seas, the rivers, and the mighty thrust of the mountains. Sometimes he took Vesper with him and discussed the relationships of men and women, plenitude, desire and fulfillment, and instructed her in the rudiments of sailing—the opportunity to press his body to hers or a stray hand to brush her breast. She knew the place Ptolemy had wanted to take us, Talley's Stand, infamous for such depravity that even the most desperate drovers stayed away.

The dark settled early now. Wind chilled our bones. Ever the surprise, Vesper guided us to a flat lay of land where other boats were pulled ashore. Bayard's Landing, she said. The town was farther along. The lights we could see in the distance were from the battery above the river where Confederate guns had guarded Almsville from the advance of Federal forces, which, when they finally arrived, were not many. A few shots had been exchanged. Weary of war, townsmen went about their business, thankful the conflict was almost over.

A dark-skinned woman named Sullivan gave us hospitality. Her home had other guests. She had only one room to offer us. The bed was wide and clean. After a pleasant supper of ham, squash, gravy, and biscuits, I lay down with Vesper on one side of me, Nandina on the other. I felt Nandina get up and come around to Vesper's side. She pushed her elbow into my ribs. I was too tired to protest. I occupied Nandina's place. Later moonlight woke me. I looked over and experienced an unexpected beatitude: Blessed are they who sleep in each other's arms.

MARTHA FOLLOWED THEO TO the rental car. "Estelle gave me this." Martha held out her arm for him to see the tiny silver harp dangling from a slim bracelet.

"Like it?"

"Very much," Martha said. "But Miss Nadir won't. She doesn't believe I should have nice things. She will be very cross with me."

Theo opened the trunk and laid Martha's suitcase beside his. "Calla will meet us at the Tampa airport."

"How far is that?"

"Two hours."

"Then we won't spend the night together?"

"We won't."

Martha got into the car and fastened her seatbelt. She wore an organdy blouse under a gray jacket. The matching skirt was short and showed off her tanned legs. A few miles later she said, "In the middle of the night, the moonlight shined in my eyes. I saw Estelle sitting in a chair."

"Watching over you?"

"I guess."

"What else do you guess?"

"She wanted to be in bed with me."

"What did you want?"

"You, of course."

"What about Pistil Pete?"

"He was in bed with me. Not all night."

"And?"

"And what?"

"And what happened?"

"He kisses better than Annabet, but that's another story."

"Let's finish this one."

"Was there more than kissing you want to know?"

"Tell me."

A sign said, REST AREA, 20 MILES. Martha slipped off her sandals, lifted her legs, and pressed her heels against the glovebox.

"Yes, yes, there was more than kissing." She brushed her hand across her knee. "Not the main event. I haven't done the man-woman thing yet. Pete got big and wet, but I wasn't ready. Besides, I didn't want him to go bragging to his friends he'd done it with me. He was sweet about it, though."

Martha watched out the window for a while. "What do people do at rest areas—sleep?"

"Use the bathrooms, buy snacks, walk their dogs..."

"So people don't stay in their cars and...you know, do stuff?"

"They could, I suppose."

"Have you ever...done stuff in a car?"

"A long time ago."

"But now you're older and wiser?"

"Older, anyway."

"I want my first time to be with a person with lots of experience. Any thoughts about that?"

"I hope you get what you want."

"Hmm." Martha smoothed her skirt over her thighs. "Theo, I'd like to have the sex thing over with. Like Pete said, people make too big a deal about it."

"You're seventeen. You have plenty of time."

"When is our flight?"

"Tomorrow morning."

"That's plenty of time. Almost every exit advertises a motel. You rent a room. We take off our clothes. We do it. We put on our clothes. We're on the road again."

"We would be different people from what we are now."

"Fine with me. I like changing. Earth mother is much kinder to her children than I imagined she would be. Besides, I think Calla is setting us up. She sent you to fetch me because she wants us to settle things between us for ourselves. We need to decide what we are to each other."

"I am your tutor, probably ex-tutor. I'm almost twice your age. You are my tutee, probably ex-tutee. That's that."

"You do sex with my mother."

"Another reason that's that."

"You, me, Calla, sounds like the making of something Greek and tragic. Do you love her?"

"We're close."

"Aren't we?"

"Not in the same way."

"In a that's-that way, you mean?"

"You know what I mean."

Martha stared out the window. "This scenery is boring."

"Are you crying?"

"Could you pull over?"

"What do you need?"

"I want to go back."

Ahead of him, down the long straight-a-way, Trooper Jenks saw a white sedan parked on the roadside. He drove past it. At the next break in the median, he circled around, and stopped his cruiser behind the sedan. The passenger's door was open, and a man and a woman stood together between the car and a drainage ditch. She was crying, and the man had his arms around her.

"Need help?" Jenks asked. The man shook his head.

Jenks noted the rental-car ID decal in the corner of the sedan's rear window. The man handed the woman a handkerchief to wipe her eyes. She smiled at Jenks. He pointed toward the ditch. "There's usually alligators," he said. The woman was barefoot. "Watch where you step." He touched a finger to the stiff brim of his trooper's hat and returned to his car. The woman was in the man's arms again.

In the morning Mrs. Sullivan had a fire burning and eggs, side meat, fresh biscuits, and persimmon jelly for our breakfast. "God knew what he was doing when he thought up those trees," she said. "War or no war, those trees don't care. They always grow us something for our use."

I asked her if she had seen much war. No, she said. Mostly plain thieving in the name of one side or the other. Sometimes she turned out guests because they were drinkers or folks of dubious conduct. A few turned against her, wanting her to show her documents, proof she was a freed woman and not some master's escaped property.

She inquired where we were bound. Vesper looked at me, I looked at Nandina. Where we might find work, Nandina answered. There were others in the room. Mrs. Sullivan stepped closer and spoke softly to Nandina. I took you for man and wife, she said. And judging from the way you caress your belly and the tender way to sit, you're carrying a new one inside you, she said and helped her hired girl take our plates to the kitchen.

I told Nandina I'd best check on our skiff or we wouldn't be going anywhere. The day being Saturday, smoking and talking, several men stood where the boats were pulled up. I looked but didn't see ours. I sensed the men were quiet now, observing me. Lost something? one of them inquired. I described the skiff I was looking for. Two men took it, he said. He pointed downriver the way we had come. There was a third man. Nice clothes, elegant boots. He had stayed in the buggy that brought the other two and left in it after they went in the skiff. Davis, I thought.

I walked back to Mrs. Sullivan's, all the while considering what choices Nandina, Vesper, and I might have. They weren't there. Mrs. Sullivan said they went off with a man in his buggy. He had paid the bill, so I didn't owe anything. I stared at her. She said, Summer, you would catch a fly with your mouth hanging open like it is.

She invited me into the kitchen. The hired girl made us coffee, good as I tasted in a while. Mr. Millsaps used to help me manage this place, but he went home to Pennsylvania to tend his mother, Mrs. Sullivan said. If I wanted work, I was welcome to stay on. I answered I would walk a bit and think about her offer. You can load and shoot, can't you? she asked. I could, I said. She being a Black woman with property near the river, there were lots of miscreants about who took it in mind to cause trouble. I admitted I didn't have a firearm anymore. She could provide one, she said. She admired the little pistol my companion had recently shot a dog with. Mrs. Sullivan had loaded again it for her.

VIII

Milo stood up and stretched. He pocketed the tin of the small Danish cigars that he bought at a smoke shop beside the state store where he acquired his whiskey and went to rouse Duncan for a bit of exercise.

"She mopes," Calla said and handed her empty cup to Mrs. Garth.

"Miss Martha was never lighthearted."

"She could be solemn, not mopey."

"She took to the outdoors, though."

"Took to it too much."

"Now you want to keep her inside?"

"Not literally."

"What are you saying?"

"I like the way Miss Nadir put it—once Martha tasted a bit of the feast the world offers, she was ready to sit down and fill her plate."

"You talking to Miss Nadir now?"

"No, I'm rephrasing what Miss Nadir told Martha and she repeated to me. Of course, Miss Nadir said it sarcastically, but at least she understood that Martha longed for something that isn't here."

"Where and what?"

"Nothing specific."

"Not Theo?"

"Not him. When she told him she wanted to go back, he thought she meant back here and back with him."

"Did you decide he wasn't her tutor anymore, or was it his choice?"

"Martha decided."

"She told him to move out?"

"Miss Nadir did."

Mrs. Garth threw up her hands. "Some phantom of Martha's imagination is in charge now?"

"I agreed with her about Theo." She had done so reluctantly. His presence created too much confusion, which could lead to conversations that no one wanted to have.

Mrs. Garth sighed and filled the dishpan with soapy water, but she spoke loud enough for Calla to hear her. "How you sleeping?"

"Don't play doctor."

"Don't need to. Like I've said before, I do the laundry. Pillows, handkerchiefs—tears dry, but like they say in country songs, they leave a trace where they have been." Mrs. Garth tried to hum the words but couldn't quite find the tune she was trying to remember.

"Then don't ask."

"Only want to make you understand."

"Understand what exactly?"

"Mr. Theo is staying at the Laurel, isn't he?"

Calla folded her hands and stared at Mrs. Garth's broad shoulders. Milo had always admired large women, country women, like the one who had agreed five silver dollars was a fair price for relieving him of his virginity. He said she was forty. He had replayed their hayloft scene is several of his books. Mrs. Garth allowed him to relive it in person. No tears on her pillow, Calla thought.

"I wouldn't do that to Martha. She does fine without Theo as long as I stay away from him too."

Mrs. Garth turned around and wiped her hands on her apron. "Send Martha to the harp woman. Let her be Martha's mother for a while."

Mrs. Garth stared at Calla. Calla stared at her empty hands as if she were helpless. "My sister..."

"Your sister what?"

"She's going to Rome for Christmas. She wants to take both of us, me and Martha."

Mrs. Garth chuckled. Martha might meet the pope and come home a Catholic. Or a nun. What would Miss Nadir think about that?"

"Who cares what Miss Nadir thinks?" Calla said.

Mrs. Garth watered the pot of chives and set it on the windowsill. The sky was low and pale. In the distance she saw Milo strolling and smoking, Duncan limping by his side. Poor animal. The new year would probably be his last. Might be mine too, she thought. So much uncertainty with Martha vanishing and returning, and the missus all shook up so that in the new year she might decide to turn her marriage around, put her house in order, which would mean no longer turning a blind eye to Milo's sexual arrangement with the help.

"Did Martha tell you what she wants for Christmas?" Calla asked.

"She said a harp."

"Told me the same. Not just a cheap beginner's model."

"You'd want to know how serious she was before spending the money."

"She's serious about McKenzie. She's who Martha wanted to go back to."

"Like I said, let her be Martha's mother for a while."

"It's not a mother-daughter relationship Martha is interested in."

"Oh...Miss Nadir must be giving Martha an earful about that."

"You and I know she only hears what she wants to hear."

The plates and glasses in the dishrack were dry. Mrs. Garth began to put them away. "Love is love. Take it where you find it."

"Wisdom from the country songs you like that you think I should impart to Martha?"

"Whether you tell her or not, eventually she'll learn it for herself."

Calla watched Mrs. Garth stack the plates carefully on the shelf. "How do you feel about Milo?"

"He's devoted to his work. I'm sorry I'm not a patient reader. I promised myself one day I would read the book he gave me. But I like holding it and believing he cared about me enough to give it."

Calla knew saying Milo had plenty of extra copies of all his books would be unkind, and she knew he did care for her. "Which book?"

"*Thatch*. What's it about?"

"The adventures of a boy named Thatch McKee. It sold well. The movies bought it and messed it up, especially the scene in the hayloft—Thatch loses his virginity to an older woman. In the book he's funny and clumsy and completely in awe of her. She's patient and almost motherly. In the movie it's dull sex. The actor who played Thatch was twenty-five, at least, and the older woman looked like she was fifteen. In real life he had had plenty of experience and didn't hide it. Same for her."

"What did Mr. Milo think?"

"The movie disappointed him, the check didn't. Plenty of money to live on while he wrote another book. Then his parents died. We moved back here. He used the money to fix the roof and the plumbing. We had talked about spending a year in Paris—France. Since being here, even Paris, Kentucky, is too far to go."

Out the window Mrs. Garth saw Milo bend down and scoop up Duncan. A minute later she heard the side door open. "I best find out if the dog has taken a chill," she said.

In the hall Milo was bent over, drying Duncan's paws with a towel. "My old friend is fading away," he said. "I'm trying to remember Kipling's elegy for his dog, but it's out of mind." He winked at Mrs. Garth. "Maybe Santa will bring me a new one—mind, I mean."

Duncan climbed into his basket, trembled, laid down, and closed his eyes. Mrs. Garth followed Milo along the hall. "If you want, I can bring you coffee."

He opened the door to his parlor and stared at his typewriter and the bottle of whiskey on the dry sink. "Eunice Garth, bring me words, lovely words, hundreds and hundreds of lovely words."

"It's Tuesday," she said. "I'll keep something warm for you."

Milo reached for his typewriter. She wasn't sure if he had heard her or not.

The cider was tasty and plentiful, like it was before the war, Mrs. Sullivan said. The drink was much requested by her guests. As the wind blew colder and the daylight ebbed earlier, fewer people required lodging. When the house was full, I slept in the stable. When it was not, Mrs. Sullivan allowed me the small room under the slope of the roof. Rufus usually occupied the space, a sullen man who barbered in a shanty in the town. According to Mrs. Sullivan, most of his customers were men accused of petty crimes who needed beards trimmed and hair washed and combed before appearing before a judge. In a scuffle with a man who would not pay, Rufus was sufficiently injured to require a doctor's care and would not return to Mrs. Sullivan's for several days.

At night, after the guests had eaten and gone to their rooms or lingered in the nook where spirits were available, the cook served me supper in the kitchen. With the house almost empty, only one couple needing attention, Mrs. Sullivan sent the cook away and served me herself, a meal of roast chicken, dumplings, and a sweet concoction made from fresh sorghum.

Mrs. Sullivan was a tall, broad-shouldered

woman with brown eyes and angular features that I thought more European than African. Was there a Mr. Sullivan? I asked. Never was and never will be, she replied, explaining how husbands were legally entitled to take for themselves all the goods and property their wives brought to the marriage. Furthermore, a woman must obey her husband's wishes and endure his tempers and moods, whether it be the cursing of his complaints, the beatings of his fists, or the crudeness of his carnal demands. She smiled and assured me that she did not speak against the pleasures of the flesh, only those who were wanton and selfish in sharing them.

I helped her do the washing up. She added a log to the fireplace in the nook and invited me to stay. Surely the aroma of woodsmoke was superior to the sour smell of the clothes Rufus left behind. She produced a handsome ship's decanter of Madeira and asked if Nandina had a husband. I answered she did. Was her child by him? I answered he believed it so. Mrs. Sullivan gave my answer some thought, then told me her body was no longer able to have children, a condition that freed the mind from care and responsibility but did not release the body from its natural longings.

Sally—as she asked that I call her—refilled our glasses, allowing me time to consider her words. Her skin glowed in the firelight. She teased me with a smile and said If I were to take down my trousers and she were to raise her skirts, the more we might find the evening to our liking. Later I confided I had never been with someone like her.

`Someone my age or someone dark? she asked. Both, I said. And did you enjoy it? she asked. Very much, I answered.`

"Milo..."

The tall clock in the hall struck five. Almost dark. Mrs. Garth had lit a fire. Milo refilled his glass and poured a drink for Calla.

"Milo, would you say you have a good imagination?"

"My readers—the handful left—would say it's worn around the edges. Why are you asking?"

"For years you have imagined us—"

"*Us,* meaning?"

"Yourself, of course, but also me and Martha."

"I sense a complication coming on. Should I sit down and suffer it?"

"Sit or stand, but I have something to say."

Milo sighed and settled into the armchair and contemplated his whiskey made amber by the firelight.

"I'm not sure when, but you retreated from me into your words, and I existed more in your imagination than I did in the day-to-day routines of marriage and raising a child. Our physical relationship became a memory. You never see us as we are—beings rather lost in the isolation of this residence. As you pointed out to me, its architect created both houses and prisons. Martha has been especially damaged. You fed her bits and scraps of stories and poems that nourished her imagination and pushed her away from the real world of school and a social life in which great poets played no part. Theo became your ally but also, ironically, the cause of her leaving your castle."

Milo nodded as if he might fall asleep. Calla took a drink and set her glass aside."Milo, you pay more attention to your characters than to Martha or me. We merely shuffle about your halls and rooms—"

"Hold on. My characters are creations of my imagination, and perhaps I do pay more attention to them than I do to you and Martha. Why wouldn't I? I'm creating them. You're already here, shuffling about my halls and rooms. Understand what I'm saying? You don't exist in my imagination."

"No, you understand—Martha and I exist, or maybe only me, in the failure of your imagination. You can't see me as anything but the woman you once loved enough to marry but not enough to love as the person she turned out to be. You can't imagine me as anything other than the woman I became. Of course, I may never have been the woman you imagined I was. As for Martha, you are very tender with her—when you give her your attention. She's a fragile vessel filled with lovely words and stories. Trouble is, she isn't so fragile anymore. She's out in the real world, but mostly she sees it though the illusions you and Theo gave her. Trouble is, there's a gritty part of her that seeks...I'm not sure how to put it."

"Seeks to taste the apple?"

Calla picked up her glass, took a long drink, and stared sadly at Milo. "Naturally, you would refer to a story, a myth. But you're right. It's not courtly love she's wants to experience. It's skin on skin all sweaty and slick and wet and sticky with desire."

"What do we do?"

"My sister and I are taking Martha to Europe."

"How does that help Martha?"

"More of the world opens for her."

"What about skin on skin?"

"She needs perspective."

"Hormones can skew the visual field. Besides, the Europe you're going to show her is culture—architecture, art, music, whatever, all the tourist things. More stories, more myths."

"She'll meet people."

"Will they provide the apples?"

"We'll make sure she doesn't choose a rotten one."

"What about Christmas?"

"You can have your castle to yourself. You can imagine Christmas any way you want it. Invite Theo and Jefferson. Perhaps the three of you can solve the mystery of Theo's ancestor."

"I already have," Milo said.

The next morning Sally's guests decided to hasten their journey home to Savannah. By noon the house was empty. Sally and I walked leisurely along the shore. Some men we encountered tipped their hats to Sally. Others, observing how close Sally and I strolled together, winced and passed without acknowledging our presence. It was not an area where women found it pleasant to be outdoors without being engaged in some obligation or task that required their attention. One woman, whose unwashed hair hung loose under her bonnet, glanced at us from the rock on which she was sitting and said to Sally, When you're done with him, let me have a turn. Farther along Sally said, She won't cost you much, but unless you have in mind forsaking your health, don't waste your money.

Evening, Sally sent the cook and the hired girl away. She set out a supper of cold ham, sweet potatoes, and a cobbler of dried cherries. We drank Catawba wine, which was much too sweet. We stacked the dishes and left them for the girl in the morning. We repaired to Sally's bedroom and lit a fire and sipped Madeira. As the room warmed, we were comfortable in fewer and fewer clothes until naked we both were, satisfying each other in a romp of pleasure. Making the beast with two backs, Sally said. Much to my surprise and delight, she had read Othello, with some difficulty, she admitted. She laughed. This time a Black Desdemona and a white Othello, she said. The role didn't fit me, I said. Aroused again, she settled on top of me. You fit perfectly where I need you to, she said.

The smoke startled both of us awake. The flames were already on the front stairs. We snatched up what clothes we could and money and some jewelry Sally had been given and escaped down the back stairs. Then there we stood, the night lit up, the bones of the house glowing with fire, the two of us almost naked like Adam and Eve awaking to a different world. The wind blew smoky specks of our paradise down the night sky.

A fire wagon finally arrived—four men and a pair of horses. The river was too far away to fill their buckets, so the men watched the fire burn itself out. Sally and I argued a ride to town in the back of the wagon. The clerk at a boarding house near the main square would rent a room to me, not to her. He agreed to let us both sleep in the stable. In the morning I asked Sally to travel north with me, but she would not. She would find the kin she had in the town and seek help or advice about the property she owned. No sense trying to keep owning it. She would sell and buy something in the Negro neighborhood. Maybe open a business. Take in laundry. Something like that. I said I wish she would reconsider. We could have a life together. We just did, she said.

I took her hand in mine and kissed her fingers.

She said, What touch and taste excites you now will change, but the color of my skin will not. Physical intercourse between the races was tolerated, but love was not. Furthermore, my passion for her would not abide, she said. Resentment would take its place. She smiled and turned away.

"Are you planning to have Christmas alone?" Mrs. Garth asked.

"Jefferson usually stops by to raise a glass with me," Milo said.

"Then what—cheese and crackers? No goose?"

"Goose was Calla's idea. Very English."

"I suppose she and Miss Martha will be dining on pasta or pizza. Very Italian."

"I suppose you and your sister will cook up a feast."

"Since Doctor Tim will be out of town and you don't need me, Mary and I probably will cook up something."

"Sounds ominous."

"We may lift a glass or two ourselves."

"Stay out of trouble."

"Mr. Milo, it's no trouble for me to leave you a meal you can heat when you're hungry."

"I can manage."

"If you could manage to leave the house, the chef at the Laurel serves a tasty country supper—local birds and venison, Mott County cornfield beans, winter squash, potatoes, breads, and pies, usually apple and pumpkin."

"Theo invited me. I said I would consider it."

"But you won't."

"I'm comfortable where I am."

"I bet Belva will be there. Probably Jefferson and Connie. She's a fan of yours. A bit of flirting—"

"Stop."

"What you should stop is your silly falling out with Wilfred Stock. You're both too old for such foolishness."

"He's too old. I'm not."

"What will happen when he's gone?"

"The Stocks shall have no root and perish from the earth. Apologies to Isaiah."

"You've lost me."

"A bit of biblical whimsy on my part. What I mean is, Wilfred is the last of his family. I have no idea what arrangement, if any, he has made for his property after he passes. Perhaps he will leave the Laurel to his cook. She's kept the business solvent. What's her name?"

"Liza Prior."

"The Black family that used to have baptisms in the Simple Creek?"

"The same. Quote me what Isaiah wrote, what you messed with."

"'Their stock shall not take root in the earth and he shall blow upon them and they shall wither and the whirlwind shall take them away as stubble.'"

"You sure carry a lot of words in your head."

"That's why I delight in my own company."

"You do talk to yourself right much."

"Then Christmas I shall have someone to converse with."

"Listen, you truly would enjoy dining at the Laurel. I wrote the number on a piece of paper and left it by the phone in the hall. Call Theo. Accept his invitation. He'll drive you."

Christmas Eve, Duncan died. Milo poured himself a whiskey and struggled to compose a eulogy.

No more the orchard, No more the rabbits and the deer. Your bones abide in earth. May your soul go clear.

A poor effort, Milo admitted. The emptiness of death had emptied words out of him. He refilled his glass and debated with himself if dogs had souls. He chose to believe they did. He found a shovel and buried Duncan near the apple tree where the dog had favored relieving himself. The sky was full of stars, so cold, so far away. Perhaps Mrs. Garth was right. Milo found her note, phoned the Laurel, and left a message for Theo.

Jefferson's Blazer had heat, Theo's Jeep did not, so he borrowed the Blazer to drive Milo to the Laurel. Dressed in a tweed suit with wide lapels and a sprig of holly in its buttonhole, Wilfred held the door open for his guests.

"Milo, been a while since I laid eyes on you."

"I'm sure you were the happier for it." Milo handed Wilfred a copy of *Thatch* wrapped in red tissue paper.

"Feels like a book. One of yours?"

"First edition. Inscribed. A cure for insomnia. One or two pages should be enough to bring on a good night's slumber."

Wilfred tucked the book under his arm and led the way to the dining room. Belva and Connie were already seated at a round table under one of the sooty chandeliers.

"Buffet style," Wilfred said. "Jefferson and the ladies have already ordered their beverages. Mason will present himself presently, gentlemen, to hear your preferences."

"To take our orders, you mean?"

"Mr. Milo, that's what I just said."

Milo sensed Mrs. Garth whispering in his ear, telling him to behave. Or maybe it was Miss Nadir. She probably didn't want to stay at the Castle all by herself.

Mason appeared, took orders, then reappeared with Theo's beer and Milo's house red, which he had selected from the choices Mason offered—house white, house red, house rosé. A cabernet from somewhere Milo decided, good enough for him to finish it and order another before everyone lined up at the buffet, which set out everything Mrs. Garth promised it would as well as trout, corn soufflé, and a beef and mushroom casserole, all ingredients produced in the county except the grapes for the wine. Milo ordered a third glass and listened to Belva and Connie swap stories about unruly customers at Dolley's. He studied Connie and remembered what it was like being her age, all the possibilities. Now he was lucky to have a ride home.

"Milo?"

"Sorry," he said. "I wasn't listening."

"Connie mentioned Martha's former tutor—Mr. Dillingham," Jefferson said.

"What about him?" Milo asked.

"Ralph had to throw him out," Connie said. "He'd been somewhere warm and came back tanned and ornery. Drank a lot, cursed Glen Campbell, kicked the Wurlitzer, cursed you, cursed your family...cursed everyone. Offered me a hundred dollars to sleep with him. Went up to five hundred before he used a word for women that Ralph won't tolerate, and he showed him the door."

"Wilfred wouldn't let him sleep here," Jefferson said, "but the sheriff had an empty cell."

Milo looked around the room and recognized no one. He had lived almost all his life in the county, but except for Professor Tripp and a couple of bootleggers, he hardly knew anyone other than people he hired to maintain the Castle.

"Wilfred wants to see us," Theo said.

Milo followed Theo and Jefferson to the front parlor. Wilfred shut the door.

Milo scanned the empty shelves. "You used to have books in here. Some valuable volumes. Where did they go?"

"Chandler Gordon, that book man in Almsville, bought them."

"He's fair."

"Fair enough, I guess. Costs money to keep the old Laurel going."

"Good crowd at lunch."

"True enough. Only two paying guests in residence, though."

"Got some that aren't paying?"

"Four-legged ones. They scurry around behind the walls at night."

"Have a few of those myself." Milo wondered if he should acquire a cat, a good mouser, instead of a new dog and eased himself into a chair by a window away from the others and closed his eyes. Theo and Jefferson chose the couch facing the bricked-up fireplace, Wilfred opposite them on the other side of a low mahogany table on which Wilfred's great-grandmother had served tea to Governor Vance, who deplored joining the Confederacy but felt compelled to do so.

Wilfred picked up the ragged ledger and rested it on his lap. "Jefferson, I found the accounts you inquired about. It's fragile, so I won't pass it around." He gently lifted the pages. "On the 9th of May—1865, of course—Chatham paid two dollars for a casket to bury the remains of a Union soldier pulled dead from the river the previous Saturday. Chatham did not record the cost of the drinks he bought for the community to celebrate the passing of the unwanted visitor."

"Delicately put," Jefferson said.

"Thing is, the man was *un*buried." Wilfred tapped the ledger nestled now in his lap. "Chatham wrote an entry for the expense of hiring someone named Lambkin to transport and deliver the casket to the family of Jerimiah Stroud in Newark, Ohio. Considering most dead soldiers were buried where they lay, or collected and buried where ground was available, going to such trouble and expense—"

"Wait. It says that—*Stroud*?"

Wilfred looked at Theo. "Most definitely."

"Jerimiah Stroud was my great-great-grandfather."

Milo opened his eyes, Jefferson and Theo leaned forward, all attention fixed on Wilfred.

"Does it tell you how much?"

"Doesn't, Jefferson. The space is blank, but must have been two hundred, or more. Chatham might not have wanted to write down the cost lest his wife find out. He put on a good show of wealth and prosperity, but bad investments and the war had lost him most of his money. Otherwise, he wouldn't have welcomed strangers into his home."

"Doesn't explain why he would send a body to Ohio. No railroad here then. Only wagons and buggies. Wasn't an easy thing to do."

"Christian duty, I suppose."

"How did he know where to send it?"

"A Bible," Theo said. "According to family history, the casket was opened. There was a Bible with the body. Despite its sad condition, they expected to recognize a feature of the Stroud they knew but did not. The Bible was wrapped tight in oilskin and stuffed into a pouch. Some water had seeped through. The pages were stained but readable. Penciled inside the cover was P. Stroud, Newark, Ohio."

"What did P stand for?" Milo asked.

"Plymouth," Theo said.

Milo smiled to himself. A man named Plymouth might have called himself Plymm. After all, *Plymouth* was a bit of a mouthful for everyday use.

"Milo, you look pleased. Memories of the fine Christmas feast my kitchen provided?"

"Scribblings Provender provided."

"Who?"

"Provender was our sheriff—1855 or thereabouts until 1873. I have some notes he made in a kind of record he kept. What he did. Expenses. What aroused his curiosity. A few names of prisoners. Comments on events or the weather."

"Sounds like something that belongs in the county archives," Wilfred said.

"A topic for another day."

"Does Provender shed any light on Mr. Stroud?" Jefferson asked.

"The sheriff noted a body recovered from the river, a Union soldier judging by his uniform trousers and belt with Union buckle. Cartridge and cap boxes were missing. No knapsack or anything else he might have carried with him. A day later a blanket roll was found in the river and a haversack, which was empty except for the Bible. Provender speculated the haversack had been found in the river by someone, who took everything out of it except the Bible, which was kept dry in a pouch like what Theo described. Might have thought keeping the Bible was bad luck. The sack itself was beat up and probably not worth keeping."

"So the sheriff assumed the Bible identified the body," Jefferson said.

"Wouldn't you?" Theo asked.

"Didn't work out, though. Plymouth Stroud is still missing. Milo, what are your thoughts?"

"It might snow."

"Milo, about Mr. Stroud."

"Ask Jefferson."

"There were two bodies, neither identified at first. The soldier in the river—Stroud or not—was wounded with a knife, at least Wells wrote he was, so he must have learned it from some source. Milo, what's Provender's part in this?"

"He recorded that a doctor named Kitts examined the body, trying to decide whether the knife wound was fatal or the river was. Then you have the body in the window, a man shot in the back and found near the river, assumed to be another Yankee, who turns out to be a Confederate named Grundy. Who shot *him*? Doubtful the man in the river did. If that person was a soldier walking home, doubtful he was by himself. Provender was sure there was a third man. Stroud probably. And probably he killed Grundy."

"Unhealthy situation to be in," Wilfred said. "Time to run."

"Easier not to," Jefferson said. "Mott County was a sparse place. Lots of men had died or survived too injured to work. Stroud could have found employment. Theo, do you know what Stroud did before he was a soldier?"

"School teacher, I've been told."

"Milo, care to weigh in?"

"Winter evenings are tedious. I prefer to waste them by myself. I need to go home."

"Apparently, Plymouth did not," Theo said.

Walking to the car, Jefferson considered the sky. "Milo, I agree. It might snow."

"And Mr. Dillingham might torch the Laurel, or try to," Milo said.

"Are you serious?"

"Wilfred turned him way. He spent a night in jail. He'll want to get even."

"Isn't what he really wants is to spend the night with Martha?"

"She won't return for a while."

"Calla told me they'd be gone for two weeks."

"Martha will stay on."

"To be with Calla's sister?"

"To be with someone. My crystal ball is too cloudy to make out a face."

"Milo, what are you talking about?"

Milo looked up at the sky and held out his hand. "'The snow In wavering flakes begins.'" The first ones melted in his palm. "The gift of prophecy is new to me. I'm not yet used to it."

"Milo, you realize alcohol can derange even the best minds."

"I was right about the snow."

"You had better not be right about Dillingham."

"Just in case, warn Theo."

❧

The week before Christmas, the bookseller near the square exhibited a selection of Bibles in his shop window, some decorated with colored capitals and bound in supple leather; some plain, but with lettering larger than the tiny print in the New Testaments handed out to soldiers. I thought about Albert giving his away and borrowing mine to start his day with scripture.

The shop's owner tapped on the window and beckoned me inside. I've seen you stop before. You have a studious way about you, he said.

The invitation pleased me. I had not the clothes for the afternoon cold. A gentleman dressed in a black coat emerged from the shadow of the shelves, holding a volume tenderly in his hand. I think this one will do, he said. He eyed me and held up an edition of Catullus. Any of him you remember? he asked. Sed mulier cupido quod dicit amanti, in uento et rapida scribere oportet aqua, I quoted. I quite agree, he said and translated for the shopkeeper, But what a woman in love says to her lover should be written in wind and rushing water.

I started to leave. Wait, he said. He paid for his purchase. I followed him outside. A light snow was falling. He inquired what languages I knew. I told him Latin and French. He asked my occupation. I answered I was employed at Carter's boarding house. I pointed across the square.

He said he had seen me recently parting most reluctantly from a Black woman. You have a keen eye, I said. Another observed you as well, he said and explained while I stood watching Sally walking away, he had been nearby discussing a business matter with a fellow who dealt with the river trade and remembered me coming ashore from a skiff belonging to a rascal named Ptolemy Green, who a day later asserted his craft was stolen by two women and a man whose description was, as we spoke, being circulated to alert the citizenry that a twenty-five-dollar reward was offered for my name and whereabouts.

My name is Plymm, I said and asked his. Henry Macintyre Elder, he answered. His employees called him Mr. Mac. For me, Henry would do. His carriage awaited at the livery stable close by. Better for me, he advised, that my face be seen in the town as little as possible. What would I lose if I were to go with him, leaving all I had carried with me at the boarding house? A razor and a few articles of clothing, I said.

From the carriage window I watched the sun slant briefly over the river far below us before the sky closed in again. Henry said he had no wife. Lucinda, his daughter, was seventeen. Perhaps I might tutor her in our national poets and whatever else interested her. Her tastes and attention changed frequently. I would find her pleasant and intelligent, but ... He broke off and did not finish what he started to say.

Chestnut trees bordered the lane to the house, a plain rectangular home-brick, three floors, a hipped roof, chimneys rising from both sides.

His late wife had inherited the property to which they moved from Richmond after the war began, foreseeing the conflict would be a greater burden to bear in Virginia than the isolated mountains of North Carolina where the scattered population spoke a language that visitors sometimes scarcely understood.

Despite frequent predations, the hogs, chickens, and the harvest of the fields had kept Henry's family fed and well. His wife was strong until the contagion of her lungs ran its sorrowful course.

Henry introduced me to Bessie, who kept the house. Jacob, her husband, had charge of the farm and livestock. Lucinda looked me over. If you have come to court me, she said, I am already spoken for. Henry informed his daughter that I was there to fill her mind, not her heart. To which she answered that God had already filled them both.

BELVA PULLED THE ROBE around her. Wind rattled the window. The glass reflected Theo sitting up in bed, a pillow behind his back, watching her. The sky was beginning to clear. She wished her mind would.

She had phoned her father. He asked the same question he had asked last year and the year before, was she ever going to quit waitressing and use her education to find a decent job again and have a future that included a husband. She had studied photography at a community college. She was qualified to sell cameras and darkroom equipment and process black-and-white film, but most people shot color, and the shop that had hired her sent color work to a lab to develop and print.

Besides, she preferred dealing with Ralph and his clientele rather than a dour shop owner and his vain and touchy customers who wanted her to praise their images, which they felt compared favorably to the work of Walker Evans or Cartier-Bresson. She did enjoy a shiver of surprise from the work of a man so small and thin she imagined he could crawl through a keyhole—black-and-whites of a tall, buxom woman dressed in bits of underwear doing mundane tasks like painting her toenails, brushing her teeth, or grooming her terrier. As for a husband—love the one you're with, like the song says? Not an answer Belva's father was happy to hear.

"Do you miss her?" Belva asked.

"Her?"

"Two hers, I suppose. Martha and Calla."

"Each in different ways."

"They'll be home soon."

"Martha won't."

"How do you know?"

"Rome will speak to her. She won't leave. She'll live with Calla's brother-in-law's family. She said they have a big house, a villa."

"A big family?"

"Aunts and uncles."

"No children?"

"The brother-in-law is a priest. Monsignor, I think."

"What will Rome say to her?

"God."

Belva breathed in the draft of cold around the window. "What about you and Calla?"

"I wouldn't have made her happy."

"You did for a while."

"That's over."

"What should I do?"

"Lie next to me."

Belva thought a moment. "Not here. Not tonight. I need my own bed."

"Need *me*?"

"My body does, but you muddle my thoughts. Ralph gave me three days off. Time to see my father."

MRS. GARTH WASN'T HOME yet. Milo was alone in the Castle. He filled a glass with whiskey and stared into the night. He glimpsed the swing of a flashlight and made out a person in a heavy coat. He opened the front door and waited. "Have you burned down the Laurel yet?"

"That's not my plan," Peter said.

"Decided to do the Castle first?"

"I want a bed for the night."

"Where's your car?"

"A mile back. Ran out of diesel. Christmas. No stations open."

"You should be celebrating with your family."

"I made it through our traditional noon meal. I'm not fond of goose."

"Are you here to cook mine?"

"I drove three hours." He took a flask out of his pocket. "I emptied it on the way. I need to sleep."

"For which you believe I will give you a bed."

"Let me be specific—Martha's bed."

"You're out of luck. She's in Rome."

"No, I'm in luck because if she were here, you wouldn't let me sleep in her bed."

"Who says I'm going to whether she's here or not?"

"Milo, please?"

Milo stepped back. Peter shuffled into the hall, shrugged off his coat, and let it heap on the floor. "Where's Duncan?"

"In the cold, cold ground."

"I'm sorry."

"He had a good life here."

"I did too, only I didn't know it."

Milo bent down and picked up the coat. "Who went with her?" Peter asked.

"Her?"

"Martha."

"Calla and her sister."

"How much?"

"How much what?"

"For a ticket—you know, to Rome."

"No idea."

"Yeah, I forgot. Calla is in charge of money."

"You were overpaid."

"I put ideas in Martha's head. They're priceless."

"If I let you sleep here, you will be gone tomorrow?"

"You're the writer. Is it 'I will be gone' or 'I shall be gone'?"

"In this case, either will do."

"Yes, I'll be on my way."

"Theo's old room is waiting for you. After he left, Mrs. Garth changed the sheets."

"She takes her time. Bet she didn't change Martha's."

"Peter…"

"Milo, think of it this way. By sleeping in Martha's bed, I save Mrs. Garth the trouble of changing two sets of sheets."

"It's not about sheets or Mrs. Garth. It's about Martha."

"Milo, she's not here."

"In your mind she is."

"Milo, it's Christmas. This is the gift I'm begging for—sleeping in Martha's bed. What's the harm?" Peter took back his coat and draped it over a chair. "Remember Thatch. He would understand."

"Don't tell me you've read the book."

"I'm more into science things, but I liked *Thatch.* I remember the part after Jane—I think that's her name—has died in the car accident, and Thatch loves her so much he sneaks into her parents' house, goes up to her room weeping and lies on her bed, hugging himself with her clothes, smelling her, imagining they were still warm from her body."

"I remember." Milo pointed toward the stairs.

"I know the way," Peter said.

Peter wasn't as drunk as he pretended to be, Milo thought and shut the door to his parlor. He replayed the afternoon meeting with Wilfred, then gently fingered the keys and began again.

A fire burned brightly and warmed the room, which was decorated with bows of pine and vines with orange berries that reminded me of the bittersweet that grew along the fencerows near our house in Ohio. Books filled the shelves. I'm afraid I collect more than I have time to read, Henry said.

He and Lucinda—I was invited to call her Lucy—sat on one side of the fireplace, and I on the other. A decanter of tawney Port on the polished table between us. Did you fight in the war? Lucy asked. Though Henry's frown gave me permission to answer or not as I chose, I said that I had and did not say for which cause. Nor did Lucy inquire. Instead, she sipped the wine Henry had served her in the small goblet and studied me as if to determine something about my situation and character.

You have a delicate way about you, she said. Did you serve as a clerk? I replied that a rifle, not a pen, had been my assignment. You are educated, though, she said. Otherwise, you should not be here ready on the morrow to discuss Emerson or Poe.

Are those your favorites? I asked. She spoke a bit of "Annabel Lee" and said she had memorized most of "The Raven." I told her I had won a contest at school by reciting "Thanatopsis." She had not heard of it. Henry set aside his wine, took down a volume of Bryant's work, and opened to the poem. She promised to read it in bed, wished us good night, kissed Henry's cheek, and carried the book upstairs.

Henry filled our glasses again. He commented that Lucy so resembled her mother that often he felt as if time had come apart and his dead wife were yet his bride and his daughter not yet born.

I recalled to him how he had described Lucy as pleasant and intelligent—which she was—but not as the beauty I found her to be. I checked myself lest I praise too keenly her eyes, her mouth, or her form so sweetly hinted by her informality of dress and the casual way she sat and moved about.

My room atop the house was small and comfortable. Lying in bed, I watched the sky out the dormer window. On such a night Nature spoke of gladness, harmony, and beauty. Most content I was, shut in and safe from all the world without.

After a morning meal of eggs, grits, and biscuits, Henry walked to the barns to speak with Jacob about the cattle. Lucy and I had the front parlor to ourselves. Bessie laid a fire and left us alone.

Lucy remarked that "Thanatopsis" was quite long. Had I really memorized all eighty-one lines? I assured her I had. And what was my prize for winning the contest? she asked. I hesitated, remembering my classmates concealing their contempt behind their sullen smiles as Mrs. Goddard, our teacher, presented me with a small, knitted sack of buckeyes. One of the older boys mumbled that it and its contents resembled something hanging between the back legs of a bull. Better than what Plymm's got between his, another boy said. Mrs. Goddard told them to leave and slammed the door after them.

Buckeyes, I told Lucy and explained what they were. And did that please you? she asked. At the time, it did, I said. Well, she said, I would have given you something better.

We were standing by the window. A trace of snow covered the ground. We counted the tracks where during the night deer had browsed the rhododendrons and azaleas planted near the house. What would you have given me? I asked. This, Lucy said, and kissed me. Speechless, I tried to concentrate on the scene out the window. What sort of tutor are you if you have not words? asked Lucy. Or have I so displeased or offended you that you are unable to express yourself?

Neither, I answered, and took hold of her hand and placed it against my chest. I have stirred your heart, she said, and pressed against me. We lingered in a longer kiss. Death was far from our minds. Any discussion of "Thanatopsis" was quite impossible.

Mrs. Garth stared at Peter. "When my sister brought me home, I thought it was your car I saw on the side of the road."

"Not happy to see me?"

"Better leave before Mr. Milo sees you."

"He invited me to stay."

"Stay or visit?"

"My car was out of fuel. Milo kindly let me spend the night."

"I wish he'd left me a note."

"A warning—watch out, Dillingham is here again?"

"What room was you in?"

"Martha's, of course."

"I didn't change them sheets yet."

"I know, and I bless you for allowing me the pleasure of her company even if I had to imagine it."

"How much pleasure we talking about?"

"A gentleman keeps those things to himself."

"I do the laundry. I know who doesn't keep what to himself."

"Anyway, I smell coffee. May I have a cup?"

"You're not a stranger. Help yourself." Mrs. Garth sat down and began to make a list of what she needed to buy at the supermarket on the Almsville Road. She didn't hear Milo enter the room.

"Any coffee left?" he asked.

"I'll make fresh," Mrs. Garth said. "On my way to the store, I can ride Dillingham back to his car."

"Leave him at the Shell station. It sells diesel. He can borrow a gallon can and have a nice walk on a sunny morning."

Mrs. Garth took the saucepan from the stove and filled a bowl with oatmeal. Dr. Tim had advised Milo to eat more than a slice of toast for breakfast. Then she left to change clothes to go to the market.

"You said you read *Thatch*. Why?" Milo asked.

"My mother recommended it. She had a column in the Raleigh paper. Reviewed your other books. She thought *Thatch* was your best."

"What's *your* opinion?"

"I haven't read anything else you wrote."

"Could you give me the short version of her conclusions about my work?"

"*Thatch* was full of feeling. The other books weren't. You could tell a good story but...I don't know."

"You don't know, or you don't want to tell me?"

"She thought you became mechanical and repetitious. In a talented way, of course."

"Of course."

The percolator's red light came on. Milo poured his coffee and sat down again. "Thatch was like me, or like what my much younger self wanted to be, a guy with lots of lovers who finally falls in love. Updike sent me a letter, said he admired *Thatch*. I suppose I wrote that self out of my system. Grew up. Perhaps your mother would say 'grew down.' How is she?"

"Morose. Drinks too much."

"And you are following in her footsteps?"

"I'm much happier—most of the time."

"Our local college lacks distinction, except occasionally for its football team. How did you end up here?"

"My high school wasn't distinguished either. I graduated because the principal didn't want to see my face anymore. The colleges I applied to didn't want to see it ever. The college here accepts anyone who pays. I like the mountains."

"Then you'll enjoy your walk. Make sure to return the can to the station. The owner is the sheriff's brother. Local law enforcement can be temperamental."

Peter set his empty cup in the sink. "You dedicated *Thatch* to J. Who was that?"

"Judy Berg."

"What was she to you?"

"You ask too many questions."

"In the book Jane is the name of the woman Thatch falls for—Jane Avery. Is Jane Judy?"

"Peter, let me repeat, you ask too many questions. Anyway, she was a long time ago."

Mrs. Garth had found Peter's coat and handed it to him. She lifted her own from the rack by the service door. "Mr. Milo, any requests?"

"Make sure to take Mr. Dillingham with you."

Peter followed Mrs. Garth outside. Her car was parked by the stack of firewood. Frost covered the windshield. "Don't turn your nose up. Pinto's a perfectly good vehicle."

"Good for junk," Peter said.

"It runs. Yours doesn't." She opened the door, found a scraper, and told Peter to use it while she coaxed some heat out of the defroster.

Peter cleared the glass and got in. The plastic seat covers crackled. "What were you and Milo talking about?" Mrs. Garth asked.

"J, the person he dedicated *Thatch* to. Read it?"

"I don't have much time for reading. Wasn't something I was ever encouraged to do, not like Miss Martha was. Who was the person?"

"Judy Berg."

"*J, Judy,* no mystery there."

"I was asking if Judy was the model for Jane, the woman in the book the Thatch character falls in love with."

"Mr. Milo told me once about feelings he had for a woman doctor. He never spoke her name, though. I heard there were women doctors, but I've never seen one. Not sure I would want a female poking and prodding me. Folks in foreign places are different."

"Like up north?"

"Don't be a smart ass." Ahead, the sun glinted off Peter's car. "It's foreign, isn't it?"

"German."

Mrs. Garth passed the car and turned onto the highway. "You love Miss Martha?"

"Probably."

"What kind of an answer is that?"

"I've never been in love before, except for a Lab I had once."

"Mr. Milo loves dogs too." The Gulf sign swayed in the wind. Mrs. Garth parked beside a pile of used tires. "Miss Martha's in Rome, Italy. Mr. Milo says she's not coming back."

"What's your point?"

"I'm asking what you're going to do."

"Buy a plane ticket."

Henry advanced a portion of my pay so I might buy clothes suitable for a gentleman—and a scholar, he added with an arch of a brow, as if he suspected the hours I spent with Lucy were not entirely given over to considerations of the writers of our young republic. When I expressed my concern, Lucy sweetly smiled and said of course her father understood I was more to her than a tutor. In fact, he would never have employed me merely to converse about scholarly topics. That I was couth and educated yet suspected of theft, and probably much more, suggested I might be useful to Henry, who, from time to time, had dealings with men of dubious occupations and morals. Had I not noticed several firearms about the house? Lucy's attraction to me, though Henry might have hoped for it, was never planned and now most welcome and approved. If Lucy and I were to wed and take up permanent residence on the property, Henry would be delighted and relieved. I admitted I would be most relieved if marriage would bring Lucy to my bed, or me to hers, inasmuch as the limitations of our daily kisses and caresses provoked an intolerable agitation to my senses. She admitted she would be relieved of a similar unease if I were to instruct her in the "arti amatoria" as I had acquired them not from books but experience.

At Easter, Minister Caldwell married us. Bessie provided a splendid supper and Henry a local brandy of subtle but substantial power. The reverend toasted us, wishing the brief interval between the bride and groom meeting and the consummation of their marriage be followed by decades of joyful devotion to each other. Henry had hired a photographer to make our picture. He requested we look at the camera not each other.

MILO PUSHED BACK FROM his writing table. He had brought Plymm to a settled place and unforeseen happiness. All morning Milo had tried to avoid the unhappiness Peter's question about Judy Berg unraveled from the skein of his memories, the loose ends of earlier days that he kept to himself and was never able to knit up and forget.

To Milo's mother, Dartmouth College and Hanover, New Hampshire, were so far from Mott County they might as well be in Canada, which they nearly were. To Milo's father, the school was an excuse for Milo to visit and indulge in the excesses of Northern snobbery without committing oneself to a life of it. One day Milo would graduate and return home. He graduated but decided to stay the summer to write.

He found a job driving a delivery truck for a prominent grocery store to support himself. The wages weren't good, but the tips were.

When the manager sent Milo to deliver an order to Dr. Berg, he assumed the doctor was at his office seeing patients and Mrs. Berg would be at home. The Bergs lived in the county. However, Judith Berg was the doctor and Mr. Berg, PhD, was an astronomer presently residing in California. The couple were divorcing. Dr. Berg—please call me Judy, she said—was taking a few weeks off to accustom herself to being single again. Today she had read, smoked a cigarette, drunk a glass of Chablis with lunch, and swum in the pond down the hill behind the barn. Dressed in snug white shorts and a loose T-shirt, she stood in the kitchen, toweling her hair. Milo had set the carton of groceries on the counter and gaped at Judy. May I offer you something—juice, water? she asked. The smudge of the birthmark above the corner of her mouth was as dark as her eyes and her hair, which framed her face. Her arms and legs were slightly red from too much sun. No, Milo finally said. He'd be on his way. Next time, he could leave her order in the kitchen. No need to knock. She would probably be at the pond or in another room assaulting the piano. She was trying to play again.

Her eyes, her smile—Milo couldn't get her out of his mind. When Dr. Berg phoned in her new order, she requested the same delivery person—*you*, the manager said as he if were surprised anyone should ask for Milo, who struck him as dreamy and distracted.

Sorry, I don't know your name, Judy said while she unpacked the contents of the carton to make sure her order was complete. Brown sugar had been left out the last time. Milo Drew, he said. She liked his long Southern vowels. Most didn't graduate from Dartmouth to delivery groceries. Shyly Milo explained he was spending the summer writing stories. Could she read one? He would try to remember to bring one next time. And where was the Cross and Blackwell's currant jelly? He'd be back with it tomorrow.

Tomorrow was Milo's day off. Judy lived four hilly miles from town. Milo didn't own a car. Hanover was small. He had never needed one. He borrowed a bicycle and set out, the jar of jelly in one pocket and a folded ten-page story tucked into the front of his jeans. A warm summer day, muggy by New England standards. He leaned the bike against the house and softly stepped into the kitchen, hoping to leave the jelly and story on the counter and sneak away without being seen.

Out the window he saw Judy returning from the pond. The sky was darker now. The breeze fluttered her shirt around her thighs. She smiled as if she wasn't surprised to see him. Great service, she said. She bent over to loosen her sandal.

Milo glimpsed her breasts under her shirt, which was blue with a frayed collar, probably something her husband had left behind. She opened the refrigerator. Chablis or chardonnay? Chardonnay, Milo said. When she reached into the cabinet for glasses, he understood the shirt was all she had on.

Will I like your story? she asked. Who do you read? he asked. John O'Hara, in the *New Yorker*. She admired his work. Mine isn't very O'Hara-ish. It's...I don't know. One of my professors called it regional. A compliment? Judy wondered. Don't think so, Milo answered.

Judy refilled their glasses. She took a cigarette from the package of Chesterfields on the shelf of cookbooks. Three a day, like Joe DiMaggio. At least that's what he told a reporter who asked how many cigarettes he smoked. Don't tell my patients, she said.

You can't be my doctor because I would know, Milo said. That's one reason, Judy said. What's the other? I don't sleep with my patients. Anything else? Milo asked. I don't sleep with anyone I'm not in love with. But—I'm not promiscuous, I just easily fall in love. Judy sipped her wine and waited. Milo, your mouth is open, she said. Words should come out.

Did you know today was my day off? he asked.

Yes, and here you are. What should we do about it?

It wasn't the sex Milo remembered, but the easy way Judy had about that and everything else. So much pleasure, so much laughter. A world unto themselves. Milo quit his job and moved in with Judy. He wrote. She read. She gardened. They ate. They drank. They swam. They sunned. They had sex. They slept. They woke, listened to the loons, and lay in each other's arms.

Douglas phoned, Judy said.

Douglas? My husband. He's coming home.

Milo tried to stay calm. But I thought…

We decided to stay together. Harvard offered Doug a position. We're moving to Cambridge. I'm going back to school, chuck internal medicine, become a psychiatrist.

Milo rented a room near Harvard Square. He started a novel, a love story. He drank and listened to Frank Sinatra sing about loneliness over and over again. The perpetual despair of the wee small hours of the morning. Milo finished the novel. He dedicated it to J. He found Judy's address, signed a copy of the book, and left it on her doorstep. He never heard from her again.

MARTHA PAUSED IN THE doorway of Milo's room and looked around. She knew Duncan was dead, but she still expected to find him somewhere in the house. "Come sit," Milo said. "In Rome did God speak to you?"

"Despite the traffic I could hear his voice all over the city, like a perpetual call to prayer," Martha said. "The monsignor had a lot to say as well. He was quite encouraging about choosing a cloistered life."

"Yet here you are."

"The cloister I'm used to. Joining another was daunting."

"And Peter?"

"Perhaps I shall meet the saint in the future—when Pistil Pete is a memory."

"A good one?"

"I'll need more experience for comparison's sake, but he was quite pleased with himself."

"Let's skip the details. Calla said he decided to stay on. Perhaps God spoke to him?"

"Whispered, perhaps. I think her name was Giulia. Miss Cielo didn't care for her. Said she thought Giulia was shady and wanted to involve Peter in something criminal. There was a fire of suspicious origin. Giulia's uncle's house in the country. She and her uncle weren't simpatico."

"Who is Miss Cielo?"

"My new friend. Miss Nadir was too inward, too superego-ish. Miss Cielo is free, open. With her the sky's the limit."

"Do you think Miss Cielo will like Theo?"

"I've already warned her that Mr. Theo will raise your hopes, then let you down."

"Leaving you to feel…what? Disappointed?"

"Incomplete. As you often said, the end is in the beginning. What began remains…"

"Unfinished?"

"Unconsummated."

"Perhaps you should give him time."

"No, time's up. Does he come around here anymore?"

"He and I and Jefferson sometimes get together."

"Mrs. Garth said the three of you met a couple of times at the Laurel and once at Dolley's."

"I wanted to show Calla I had a life beyond the Castle so she could have her own. What can you tell me about the man she's interested in?"

"A publisher. Likes opera, wine, and strong coffee. Speaks English."

"Sounds like a winner. Do you want to stay here or return to Italy with her?"

"I want to learn to drive and have friends other people can see. Professor Tripp can arrange for me to take courses at the college. Maybe a creative writing seminar."

"Let me warn you that writing fiction means living with people only you can see. You hope one day readers will see them too."

Martha stood up and hugged her father. "Perfect," she said.

IX

Ralph scowled at Milo. "You're getting to be a regular."

"You don't sound happy about that."

"Winter months I'm grateful to have any customers. Had to give Connie and Belva time off. Euni Garth not satisfying your needs, so you come here?"

"You know Eunice?"

"Seems like forever. I used to drive a school bus. I watched her grow up. I'd quit though by the time she dropped out and went to work learning cooking from Miz Prior at the Laurel. Heard Euni was good at that and at some other things best not spoken of."

"Still is," Milo said.

"Her great-granddaddy started the sawmill in the county after the war."

Milo pushed his empty glass across the bar. "What war?"

"The one that caused your ancestor to build that fortress you live in."

"It provided three years of work for half the county."

"That's an exaggeration, but you're mostly right."

Ralph started to pour Milo another drink. "I'll wait for Theo and Jefferson," he said.

"What's the topic tonight?"

"A woman who came to see Sheriff Provender."

"For sure that was a while ago."

"About two years after the war you just mentioned."

Ralph nodded toward the door. "Those gentlemen you spoke of have arrived."

The Wurlitzer was on winter break. The owners of the feed store and the propane company were the only other customers. Ralph handed out menus and took drink orders. He served Milo and Jefferson their whiskeys and Theo's beer and lingered to hear Milo tell them about Provender's visitor.

"Provender wrote down his expenses to travel to Holcombe County to confer with the sheriff there. A woman accused a man Provender knew as Noble Davis of owing her father a thousand dollars, which he now owed her, and she hoped to use Provender's persuasion to collect the debt. An intruder had shot both her father and husband and set fire to their house. The man locked her in a bedroom and left her to perish, but she climbed out a window and escaped down a rope ladder. The house servant and her husband were in the barn. They were unable to contain the fire. The bodies were burned and no longer recognizable. The woman had fled with a tintype of herself and her husband, who Provender wrote 'pricked my interest.'"

Milo paused to taste his drink. Ralph sat down to listen.

"Why?" Jefferson asked.

"Provender recognized the husband in the picture. He had seen him in town. He was suspected of stealing a skiff. Maybe shooting a dog. Some confusion about that. For sure, though, two women with him had disappeared."

"Then what?"

"Apparently, the Holcombe County sheriff verified what the woman said. Provender later records that he received fifty dollars as a reward for assisting her in collecting what Davis owed."

"Owed for what?"

"Don't know," Milo said.

He didn't but he did. Mrs. Garth peeked in and asked if he wanted company. Tomorrow, he said, and pulled the typewriter closer.

After breakfast Bessie had gone to the barn to talk to Jacob, who had been feeling poorly. A visitor rapped on the door, the knob of a walking stick from the sound of it. When I opened the door, Davis pointed a pistol at me and summoned Henry, who said if Davis had come to pay him his one thousand dollars, a firearm was unnecessary.

Davis explained he had had difficulty finding me, but now I was found I was to repay the money he had given me to father Vesper's child as well as a substantial penalty for assisting Nandina to run away. If I did not hand over one hundred dollars immediately, I was obliged to accompany him to a lodging where we might reach agreement to how I would discharge my debt, otherwise he would discharge the pistol aimed at my skull, resulting not only in my demise but also an unsightly stain in a room obviously decorated and kept with care. Henry said Davis would do no such thing. He sent Lucy upstairs and told her to lock her door.

Henry, always suspicious of visitors and armed for trouble, reached into his coat pocket on the pretext of giving Davis what money he had on him on my behalf. Instead, he drew his own pistol, which was as small as the Derringer Nandina had carried in her reticule. There is one more, Davis said, the cue for Tates, armed with his own weapon, to join us. He staggered a bit and raised the weight of his revolver unsteadily in his hand.

Henry fired first, then Davis, then Lucy, who had returned from upstairs with another of the weapons Henry kept prepared for unpleasant visitors. Tates toppled backward, Henry forward, reaching out as if to touch Lucy one last time, knocking the lantern off the table, spilling its oil, on which fire flashed and quickly spread. Davis pressed his coat against his wounded shoulder and ran from the house.

Later Lucy showed me the wedding picture she had saved. She lamented her poor aim that allowed Davis to survive, which the house did not. According to Lucy's account of events, I, who was safely sheltered by Reverend Caldwell, who had married us, had also perished, thus there were two remains uncovered when the embers had cooled sufficiently to be raked and explored, two shapes of charred flesh and bone, the remains of her husband and her father. If Davis wished to implicate himself or reveal his purpose for visiting Henry, so be it.

After Lucy, with Sheriff Provender's persuasion, had received the sum Davis owed her father, she gave the money and Henry's two mules to Bessie and Jacob to get them back to relatives in Georgia. Often I had imagined returning to Ohio, but now I—Plymm—was interred close by Henry and his beloved wife, all my sins forgotten.

The open road lay west. Can you still recite "Thanatopsis" complete? Lucy asked. I affirmed I could. She inquired about Emerson's poems, the ones she admired especially—"To Rhea" and "The Snow Storm." Yes, I knew them and some of Longfellow, Whittier, and, of course, Mr. Poe.

Thus we chose to journey. Lucy has a lovely voice and performs the songs people love. "Beautiful Dreamer" and "Jeanie with the Light Brown Hair" are the most popular. I recite verse that I hold dear. Here and there I acquire a new volume and more words to add to my repertoire, sometimes shamelessly adding my own. Lucy ends our performance with "Amazing Grace."

Most everywhere we encounter the fervor of spiritualism, and all manner of testaments about communicating with the dead, many of them the buried and unburied victims of the war. In Tennessee a man described a pair of women who spoke joyously of spirits longing to welcome our eternal presence when death released us from the prisons of our bodies. The man described the women. Vesper and Nandina, I thought. A child with them—he did not recall her name—shone with glory, he said.

The ways ahead are many. Perhaps our paths will cross, and I may behold the child myself. If not, I shall not complain. I have survived where others have perished.

I call myself James, and if a surname is required, then I sign Elland. What follows is the narrative of our adventures—Lucy's and mine.

Dolley's was crowded. "I'll get refills," Jefferson said, leaving Theo and Milo by themselves while he carried their empty glasses to the bar. Connie promised their burgers and pizza would be out in a minute.

"I've given up," Theo said. "I assume Plymouth Stroud died

and was buried or lived and never wanted to go home." He waved across the room to Ralph. "Not sure I do. Wilfred wants me to run the Laurel. What about you—your work?"

"I've made a start. Adventures await. My characters are always wandering ahead of me. I'm trying to catch up."

Theo closed his eyes and listened to Patti Page lament losing her darling again. "The Castle must feel lonely. Keeping company with anyone besides Mrs. Garth?"

"Miss Nadir nags me with questions."

"Like what?"

"Why do I keep doing what I do? She takes a dim view of my work."

"What do you tell her?"

"I say I'm trying to write my way back to where I started."

"Where was that?"

"A room above a bakery. I lived on peanut butter and stale bread. Cats peed in the hall. Children shouted in the street. Students with bookbags slung over their shoulders slouched their way to Harvard Square. Rain streaked the window. Trees shed their leaves. I smoked Chesterfields. Sinatra and I lamented the wee small hours of the morning. He was much better at it than I was. He sang and sang. I wrote and wrote. A very long love letter. I never heard from the woman I sent it to. Some reviewers liked it." Milo shrugged. "I suppose once I started, I kept on going. As much as anything, writing keeps my soul together."

"But you enjoyed good times—California sun, celebrity, money," Theo said.

"The sun out there never seemed real. It was always as if a set decorator put it in the perfect place. Here it's different. Out there the days are always full of the future. Here it's the past. Out there people forget who they are and invent who they want to be. I'm groping for the person I used to be."

Jefferson brought a tray with three full glasses. "Did I miss anything?"

"Wilfred asked Theo to take charge of the Laurel."

Jefferson tasted his whiskey and looked at Theo. "Going to do it?"

"Belva thinks I should."

"What do *you* think?"

"The place is falling apart."

"It's a landmark—full of history," Milo said.

"Plus rot and rodents, dust and decay."

"Theo, easy on the alliteration. That's my department."

Connie appeared with the dinner orders. "You and Ralph working alone tonight?" Jefferson asked.

"Wilfred invited Belva to have supper at the Laurel."

Jefferson glanced at Milo. "What are we to make of that?"

"Anything else?" Connie said. "Extra ketchup, mustard?" The men shook their heads. She walked away.

Jefferson leaned across the table. "Theo, what aren't you telling us?"

"Wilfred wants Belva to know what it was like growing up at the Laurel."

"Why would she want to know about Wilfred's childhood?"

"She doesn't."

Jefferson put down his pizza. "Milo, you spend your time imagining peoples' lives. What's going on?"

"I suspect Miss Belva is with child."

Jefferson stared at Theo. "Yes?"

"Yes," Theo answered.

Milo warned Jefferson to stop shaking his head or he would addle his brain, which was already stressed enough. Then Milo turned to Theo. "If it's a boy, I wouldn't name him Plymouth. People will associate him with a rock or an automobile."

"Any suggestions?"

"Plymm is a name that comes to mind."

"What kind of name is that?"

"Provender scribbled it in his book—the name and a question mark. That's all I know."

About the Author

Christopher Brookhouse is the author of numerous works of poetry and fiction, among them *Running Out*, which earned the Rosenthal Award from the American Academy of Arts & Letters; *A Selfish Woman*, nominated for the National Book Award; and *Fog, the Jeffrey stories*, winner of the biennial New Hampshire fiction prize.

His most recent works include a 4-book series about aspiring writer-turned-sheriff Gus Salt, set in post WWII North Carolina: *A Pinch of Salt*, *Percy's Field, Nolan's Cross*, and *A Mind of Winter; Messing with Men*, a story of old murder and the colliding lives of three retirees on an island in Florida; and *How It Was*, the story of a young man hired by the athletic department of a small Southern college to tutor a superb Black basketball recruit—and gets ensnared in a variety of academic and local conspiracies.